RADIO BOY

CHRISTIAN O'CONNELL

Illustrated by Rob Biddulph

HarperCollins Children's Books

To my mum and dad, Liam and Jenni. Thanks for always encouraging my dreams and never laughing at them, even when they included becoming:

- *Boxing middleweight champion of the world*
- *World BMX champion*
- *A DJ*

If your parents laugh at your dreams, sack them.

CHAPTER 1

FIRED!

'You're fired.'

I stared at the man sitting opposite me. The programme controller of St Kevin's hospital radio. Barry Dingle, or 'Bazza' as he insisted we call him. No one ever did.

'What?' I said. 'But I haven't done anything wrong.'

'I . . . I know that, Spike. But you can't work here any more. I'm sorry.'

What kind of a man sacks an eleven-year-old boy from his dream job? A monster, that's who.

'*Why?*' I spluttered. Later, on the bus home, when I replayed this moment in my mind (as I will do for the rest of my days), there were many things I wished I'd said to the bald-headed man ruining my life. Such as:

1. You're a monster.
2. Technically, you can't actually fire me as I'm a volunteer.
3. My mum said you live in your mum's basement. Who's the bigger loser here?
4. Have you got any tissues as I think I'm going to cry?

A MONSTER

But I didn't say any of that. Annoyingly, my face was letting me down. My bottom lip had started to wobble, and my eyes flooded with tears. The tears of a dreamer who'd just had his heart RIPPED out, put into a blender and then force-fed back to him. My fantasy of being a famous DJ with a detached house and gravel driveway (and personalised gold-plated headphones) was no more.

Barry Dingle was firing me from the only hour of joy I had in my life, my radio show.

The *Wacky Kids' Wonder Hour*, Saturday mornings at 6am. Maybe the name of the show hadn't helped. For the record, it came from 'Bazza', not me. But I loved doing that show. It was sixty minutes when for once I felt I was funny and good at something. It was the highlight of my week.

Well, it had been.

Sure, it was only hospital radio, and most people don't even know hospitals have their own radio stations. But they do: run, for the most part, by overly enthusiastic volunteers with bad breath and sandals. The thing was, I'd read in all the interviews with my favourite DJs that they'd started off in hospital radio. I collected these interviews in a special folder under my bed, safe from my sister's prying eyes. Codenamed 'My Favourite Stamps'. I'd learned my lesson after she found a notebook I'd been practising my autograph in.

I thought I was following in these DJs' footsteps. Not any more. Me getting fired was also going to be bad news for the fellow members of our AV Club at school. The AV (Audio Visual) Club is an after-school club run by Mr Taggart. There are only three members: me and my best mates, Artie and Holly, and each week Mr Taggart does his best to school us in the magical worlds of broadcasting, video and print.

There had been a fourth member, Dave Simpson, but he quit for Jazz Club. We could hear them practising, and I'm no expert, but it sounded like they were all playing from diffcrent pages in different books.

I liked to think I was held in some regard by Mr Taggart and the AV Club, as I was actually *doing* radio. Spike Hughes – the country's youngest radio DJ.

Now I was the youngest *sacked* radio DJ. A scandal like this could ruin the AV Club. I just hoped we were strong enough to survive.

The bald-headed monster man started to speak again, his coffee-flavoured breath hitting me in the face. Ugh.

'It's awkward, Spike, and I feel dreadful having to do this face to face. I was going to tell your mum, but . . .'

He drifted off, a thousand-yard stare appearing in his eyes. This was a look I'd seen a million times when people said the '*M*' word.

Mum.

It was the look of fear, and my mum was the source of it. A force to be reckoned with. Confident, protective – *very* protective – and always on the lookout for possible danger in everything around me and my sister. She's a ward manager at the hospital and that's how I got the show. My mum 'persuaded' Barry Dingle to give me an hour on the radio. Her ability to get people to do what she wants is, according to my dad, 'nothing short of a superpower'. Running a hospital ward is the ideal job for my mum. It puts her in charge, looking after people, and it provides her with an endless supply of grisly stories to justify her need to protect us from the modern world.

'See, just today we had a boy come in who got a skateboard for his birthday. Yes, it seemed like fun to him, Spike, for the two minutes before he fell off . . . Now he only has one eye, one leg and no arms. They have to pull him around everywhere on the skateboard.'

No, Barry Dingle wouldn't have dared give my mum this news or she would have done something to him that would've made him a patient at St Kevin's. I'm not saying she would've physically hurt him. No. She would've made him hurt *himself*, using her special powers.

Bazza started to clear his throat to bring his attention back to the job in hand: sacking me.

'You know I like you, Spike, and you're a talented kid; you're a bit odd but I don't mind that. It's just that we've got the results back from our yearly audience review. It tells me which shows are the most popular and which aren't . . . and that leads me to your show . . . I'll just come out and say it . . .'

'What?' I snapped, defensively.

'It has no listeners. Actually, that's not true — there was one.'

'Well, that's good; you always said the key to radio is to imagine you're talking to just one person,' I reasoned.

'Yes, but it turns out that one person was an elderly lady called Beryl who had sadly passed away and no one turned her radio off. Tragic really.'

Oh.

'Look,' Barry went on, 'I can't justify your kids' show any more. The show after you, *Graham's Gardening Gang*, is our biggest by far so I'm extending his slot by an hour.'

This was even worse news. The shame of it. Graham Bingham is a really patronising old man with a huge beard that has bits of food in it, and on one occasion I think I saw a small mouse in there. Graham actually resembles a garden gnome. All that's missing is a red hat and a fishing rod.

I was being sacked and replaced by a show about allotments and hedges, presented by a gnome.

'When's my last show?' I asked, thinking at least I could have a big send-off.

'You've just done it.'

And that's how my career in radio ended. The dream was over. Part of me wished it had never begun. How cruel to be given hope and then have it taken away. By a gardening show. My dad always said supporting England at football was like this.

'It's the hope that kills you, son.'

As I was packing away my headphones, I saw something in the bottom of my bag. A gift Artie had got me from his recent holiday to France. Stink bombs. Banned from our school after some boys threw them into the staffroom. Poor Miss Mills fainted into the eager arms of the PE teacher, Mr Lewis. (Quick update on this: they've just returned from their honeymoon.)

No, I couldn't, I thought.

Yes, I could. I really could.

'Sorry, Bazza, I've left my keys in the studio. Can I just pop in and get them?' I asked, innocently.

'Yes, of course, Spike. It's a tulip special this week. Graham's just setting up.'

Indeed he was. Graham and his garden show, now extended by an hour. As I walked past all the hospital supplies, I saw Graham and his beard were in the studio, sorting through some tulip bulbs.

'Ah, Spike, so sorry to hear about your show. No hard feelings, lad. You're young, you'll be fine. Probably too young really to have a show, much to learn still. Hey, stick around and help out on my show if you like – see how it's done!'

With that, Graham let out a loud cackle and stroked his beard. As I said goodbye and walked past the flowerpots and compost he'd brought in, I placed not one, not two, but three stink bombs around the studio. One for each hour of his newly extended show. My gift. The barely audible crunch they made as I left the studio, treading on them, will always be the greatest sound I'll ever hear. No, second. The best was a few minutes later when Graham's theme tune started playing. As he began discussing the merits of Dutch tulips, all that could be heard was the sound of a human gnome coughing violently and swearing at the top of his booming voice as he threw up into his beard.

I later found out that as a result of some complaints (from my mum) about his language, they had to move Graham's show to the graveyard slot.

1–4am.

CHAPTER 2

Gateaux chateau

I sprinted up the steps out of the hospital basement, fleeing the scene of the dreadful crime. The crime of Barry Dingle killing my radio career. I walked past the dozing security guard. Quite why there was a security guard at the hospital always puzzled me. Was someone trying to steal the patients? What would they do with them? Sell them on eBay? I was about to hand in my security pass when I thought better of it.

You never know when that might come in handy one day.

St KEVIN'S HOSPITAL
Spike
HUGHES
Hospital radio
650 854-77 SHughesx

I then began my very own solemn walk of shame to the bus stop. Like a funeral march. Same as when our dog Sherlock is told off for trying to steal food from the dinner table. His ears go back, his tail drops between his legs and he skulks away, hugging the ground. My walk of shame quickly turned into the bus ride of shame, as I got on the Number Nine as usual to head back to the estate I live on.

At least now I could relate to all those famous people I read about in my sister's celebrity magazines. The ones with headlines like 'WASHED-UP STAR NOW CLEANS CARS'.

I asked myself, *Did I crash and burn too young?*

I didn't want to go back home right away as I wasn't ready for my mum's interrogation. (I was already imagining it: 'So you said what to him? Then what did he say? Why didn't you call me immediately? What *exactly* did he say?')

Dad would try to fix the situation, but this time he wouldn't be able to, as it was broken forever. No, at a time like this I needed the kind of people who wouldn't ask five thousand questions or try to make it better. I texted my best friends, Artie and Holly.

> Calling emergency meeting of the AV club. Meet at Artie's in half an hour. Come alone.

This was a devastatingly serious situation so I used no emojis.

There isn't an emoji for 'I've been sacked by a bald-headed monster and set three stink bombs off, causing a studio evacuation'. If there was, maybe it would look like this:

I suggested meeting at Artie's as I knew he'd be in. He's in every Saturday morning after returning from his weekly pilgrimage to Lionel Vinyl with a fresh batch of records. Artie loves music, but only if it's on vinyl. These are round discs of black plastic that songs used to be played on in olden times. To me they look like something you'd see in a history museum next to an Egyptian mummy or a dinosaur tooth. It makes no sense that when the rest of the world is simply beaming songs from outer space on to their phones in nanoseconds, Artie is spinning black plastic discs. It's like preferring to drive an old horse and cart rather than a Ferrari sports car. Or using a carrier pigeon to send a message to your parents asking them to pick you up from the swimming pool, instead of just texting them.

Artie discovered his dad's old record collection last year when he found him stuffing the discs into bin bags for the guide dogs' charity shop. Those dogs are amazing. I love my dog Sherlock too. My sister wanted a cat and I was desperate for a dog. Cats are scary to me. They will attack you at any moment with no warning. What an awful pet. If you had a mate who suddenly just tried to scratch you, you would not say he or she was 'cute'. Dogs are way cooler and help blind people. There are no guide cats.

Anyway, I won the dogs vs cats debate and Sherlock became the fifth member of our family. However, it was a short-lived victory as my sister used all this to get what she really wanted: a pony.

It cost way, way more and means we won't have a foreign holiday this year.

Anyway, as Artie's dad was cramming these antique relics into his work van, Artie asked what they were. While his dad told him, an instant obsession was formed. Artie took them back into his house and – fast-forward a year – he loves nothing better than sitting in his bedroom, listening to his records on his headphones.

If Artie robbed a bank, maybe to fund more record-buying, and I had to describe him to the authorities, I'd say he looked like an owl. Big eyes, thoughtful and a large rotational head. I made that last bit up, but he does sometimes cough up pellets. This might be from all the out-of-date cakes that are freely available in his house. That's the big bonus if your parents own a bakery empire. Every time I go round, I'm offered a wide variety of cakes, and it's guaranteed all of them will be out of date. Artie's parents own about five cake shops all over town, under the name Mr Cake. Much to Artie's horror, sometimes his dad makes him dress up in a giant cupcake costume as the shop's mascot – 'Mr Cake' – handing out freebies in the High Street at the weekend.

Artie is accidentally funny. He just says stuff. There isn't any filter, or any kind of pause, to think about what he is saying. As a result, other kids at school reckon he's a bit odd. Like the time he was sent to the headmaster, Mr Harris, after our English teacher, Miss Tusk, asked the class to describe her. Artie shot his hand up, she nodded at him to speak and he said, 'Skin like a ham slice.' I don't think it was what she was after.

Artie's detached house is just on the outside of the estate Holly and I live on. His parents are way richer than mine. We live in a semi-detached house, but Artie's house doesn't have any other house attached to it. Also, he has a gravel driveway. I think my dad might be jealous because whenever I mention Artie's house my dad immediately snaps back with, 'Paid for by kids' rotten teeth from all those cakes; might as well have kids' teeth in his driveway instead of gravel!'

Artie goes on two foreign holidays a year to exotic-sounding places I've never heard of. He also goes skiing every year. The closest I ever came to an Alpine trip was when it snowed last year and Dad made me a toboggan. When I say 'made me', it was an old door cut in half. I had the half with the door handle.

Holly's house and my house have numbers, but Artie's house has its own name. Artie's house is called 'Gateaux Chateau'.

The estate Holly and I live on was built in olden times (1970-something) when the people whose job it was to come up with street names finally ran out of ideas.

I imagine the meeting went like this:

'OK, what can we name all the streets after?'

'Queens, you know, like—'

'Done that.'

'Kings?'

'Done.'

'What about birds? Sparrow? Kestrel—'

'GENIUS! Let's take the rest of the day off to celebrate how good we are!'

Holly is on Chaffinch Close and I drew the short straw with Crow Crescent.

I got off at my stop. I was going to get my bike and cycle over to Artie's. No one was at home, but as I was leaving with my bike I saw Terry. Sensei Terry. He made me LEAP right out of my skin as he was crouched behind our garden wall at the front of the house.

'Sorry, Spike,' said Sensei Terry as he stood up. 'I heard a noise and, seeing your dad's car wasn't here and fearing a burglary, I came to investigate. Happy to see it's you.'

'Yes, just off to my mate's.'

'Safe on the roads, Spike. Safe on the roads.'

Sensei Terry muttered to himself as he turned away, going back to scanning the road like a robot.

Sensei Terry, on top of being our postman and a karate instructor (which is why he insists on being known as Sensei Terry), also runs the local Neighbourhood Watch. He lives four doors down from us. When he isn't working or teaching karate, he seems to be permanently patrolling our streets and area for any, and I mean *any*, suspicious activity.

Like the time he called the police to our neighbours' house as their curtains were still closed at lunchtime one Sunday. The police gave the Meachers the shock of their life as they kicked down their front door, splintering it into a thousand pieces, screaming, *'POLICE! PUT YOURS HANDS UP NOW!'*

Only to find a terrified Mr and Mrs Meacher,

who had been enjoying a nice lie-in after a late night celebrating their fiftieth wedding anniversary. Sensei Terry was made to pay for a new front door and was cautioned by the police. For the second time that year.

The first time was a classic. Sensei Terry called the police to report 'terrorist activity' at Number 56 Crow Crescent. The home of a family Sensei Terry hated, as the dad was a rival martial arts instructor.

'He teaches kung fu; it's not a patch on karate, just Mickey Mouse stuff you see in movies,' Sensei Terry would confide to anyone at every opportunity.

The police obviously take these calls very, very seriously. A SWAT team was dispatched and officers with guns stormed the Woodses' house. They were led out in handcuffs. An emotional Mr and Mrs Woods and their two teenage daughters protested their innocence tearfully.

'They're trained to behave like that – they're lying,' said Sensei Terry, who was watching it all round at ours. Next to my mum, by her go-to observation post. Just behind the net curtains.

Four ski masks were removed from their house, which Sensei Terry had seen them all in and presumed them to be planning a terrorist attack, rather than what they were actually doing, which was trying on some new ski gear ahead of their trip.

Now Sensei Terry turned to look at me again, frowning. 'You OK, Spike?' he asked. 'You look down.'

I swallowed. 'Fine, fine, Sensei Terry,' I said. You see, there are only two members of the Neighbourhood Watch and my mum is the other one. She and Sensei Terry give each other 'intel' on a daily basis. Anything I said to him would get back to her, and I did *not* want my mum knowing about me getting fired. Who knew what she would do.

'All right then,' said Sensei Terry. 'But if you're ever in any kind of trouble, you let me know, OK? There's a spare place in my karate class, you know.'

'OK,' I said.

'You would learn the ancient art of KARATE, thousands of years of wisdom for just four pounds a week. Think about it, Spike.'

No, I won't, Sensei Terry.

'Sure,' I lied.

CHAPTER 3

I'm an O-list celebrity

I cycled to Artie's house and when I got there Artie's dad, Ray, aka 'Mr Cake', answered the huge oak door (with bronze cake-shaped door knocker) halfway through eating a bun.

'Spike! You look sad – everything OK? Come in.' I think that's what he said anyway. It was hard to fully understand with all the cake in his mouth.

'I've been sacked from my radio show,' I said

glumly. Just saying those words out loud caused a pain in my heart like I'd never felt before.

'WHAT! Why? Did you play some of Artie's records and put them all to sleep?' Mr Cake said, still chewing that bun.

'I don't have any further comment at the moment,' I answered. I'd heard troubled celebrities say this when hassled by the paparazzi. Mr Cake laughed out loud at this and a load of crumbs came flying out.

Sure enough, Artie was upstairs in his headphone heaven. His parents had converted the loft into a hangout for their only child. Up there was a massive TV about the size of our dining-room table and a pinball machine. The walls were lined with hundreds of records. Artie's collection was more like a record library. Radio stations would have less. Most stations only seem to have one CD actually, as they just play the same songs over and over.

I walked over, yanked one of his headphones dramatically away from his ear and yelled, 'THEY SACKED ME!'

Then I collapsed on to his bed. Artie stopped the record he was listening to. This he had to do with care and precision. You'd think he was a nuclear scientist handling plutonium and any sudden movement might blow the whole world up. Really, though, all it involves is lifting a needle from the record on the turntable. All in the time it takes to get your shoes on. When he could have just pressed PAUSE on his phone.

'Spike, what are you talking about?' Artie said as he stood over me.

'Apparently, no one listens to my show.' I put my head in my hands. I told him exactly what had happened, sparing no details. The owl took it all in. Then spoke.

'So . . . you just give up now? Where's the fight in you? Gone, just like that? Can't mean that much to you then.'

'I've been *fired*. From a volunteer job on hospital radio. How will I ever be a radio star now?'

'By not giving up,' said Artie.

'Who's giving up?' said a voice from behind us.

My other best friend had arrived. She has a habit of appearing out of thin air. It's as if she lives in another dimension and is beamed into our world from time to time. Her earth name is Holly. Elf-like in appearance, with piercing blue eyes that see right through you. My mum once said – a bit cruelly – that her ears stick out so much she 'looks like a monkey'.

However, no one would ever say anything like this to Holly's face as that would be a HUGE mistake. Holly may not be one of the super-popular girls at school, but she is seriously tough. A brown belt in karate, she even takes part in big competitions and is unbeaten in eight fights. I once asked her why she didn't use her skills on the kids at school when they made monkey noises behind her back.

She looked at me intently and said, 'The first and most important lesson Sensei Terry teaches you is when *not* to use martial arts; it's about self-control, Spike.'

No idea what that meant. If it was me, I'd have karate-kicked Martin Harris, the school bully, all the way down our high street. Of course, it wouldn't be me because you couldn't pay me to go to Sensei Terry's karate class. Despite all my mum's attempts to get me to 'join in', I don't like any kind of activity that involves sport or being in a group. Apart from AV Club. But that's different.

I'd also say Holly is probably the smartest out of all of us. Top of the class in science. I think she even knows more than the teacher. I don't know any other kid who can use a soldering iron. She used it to repair the AV Club printer. Her dad, Timothy Tate (*'Please, Spike, call me Tim'*), is an inventor. Just not a very successful one. All around their house are empty bits of circuit boards and the wiry guts of computers. In the shed, it's like a graveyard of his failed inventions.

Personally, I liked his singing kettle that stopped singing when it was boiled. Sadly, it only 'sang' one song so people got fed up with it and it was voted Most Irritating Product of the Year. This was made worse by the fact that the number-two place on the list was taken by another of his ideas, a pillow that cut your hair as you slept. This ended up on the teatime news, with buyers of the

Pillow Barber complaining that not only were random bits of their hair missing, but also bits of their ears too. Two hundred Pillow Barbers now rest in pieces in the shed under a blanket, as if hiding their shame from the world.

As I've already said, me, Holly and Artie are the only members of the AV Club. None of us will ever be one of the cool kids at school. Life has just decided it. I'm not saying we aren't all *great kids* (as my mum is always telling me), but being 'cool' is like being an A-list star in those celebrity magazines. These A-listers may not be the smartest or even the prettiest, but they are the chosen ones and they get to walk on the red carpet.

Holly always says, 'Who cares? We're not one of the pinheads. Good.'

I'm not so sure. Sometimes I quite fancy a walk on the red carpet. I'd secretly hoped the radio show might bump me up a few letters in the celebrity alphabet to at least the O-list or the M-list. This would mean the girl of my dreams who I was going to marry, Katherine Hamilton, would not only talk to me, but not mind being *seen* talking to me. She's red carpet. I'm the kind of carpet your nan and grandad have that looks like someone's been sick on it every day for the last fifty years.

Artie, Holly and me go way back. Our mums have been friends since they met in birthing class. They bonded instantly over a love of gossip, fixing other people's lives and elasticated maternity pants. The three of them are a powerful union. The league of mums.

Anyway, back to the story unfolding in Artie's room.

'I've been sacked from my show,' I said to Holly.

'Well, proves what an idiot that programme controller is,' she said. 'That's why he isn't working in a proper radio job. Running his fake station. Loser.'

'Um. Yeah,' I said.

'Doesn't mean you're not a great radio presenter,' continued Holly. Her head jutted forward to really drive the point home.

The three of us chatted it over before I had to ask one final question.

'Please be honest: do you want me to resign?' I said.

'From what?' said Artie.

'The AV Club. I've been fired from an unpaid radio job. I've brought shame on you both.'

Holly rolled her eyes. 'Spike. If you quit, then you're not my friend any more. Only losers quit. I'll kick your backside if you do and put you on your mum's ward.'

'But radio's my thing,' I said. 'The only thing I want to do. The only thing I'm good at. What am I meant to do now?'

'Well . . .' said Artie. 'We've been promised a school radio station for ages. Why don't we ask again about it?'

'Yeah,' said Holly. 'No more being fobbed off. We'll show them the petition again. And you can present. You'll be back on the radio in no time. I mean, no one else in the school has your experience, do they? I'll make a list of action points.'

Holly is super-organised and loves making lists.

That's what friends do. Lift you up when you're down. And offer you out-of-date cakes.

CHAPTER 4

'Pirate party in my pants'

The wafting aroma of pony poo told me I was nearly back home at 27 Crow Crescent.

Dad's car would be caked in the stuff after taking my sister to some awful pony gymkhana. For those of you lucky enough not to know what a gymkhana is, it's like a strange kind of sports day for ponies. All watched and cheered on by people with names like Tamara and Fenella.

One day last summer I was made to go to one

of these events and help out. Worst day of my life. I was forced to wear a high-visibility jacket that would have been too big for a giant, and run the car park. It got even worse when Katherine Hamilton, the girl of my dreams, turned up with her mum. No girl is impressed by anyone in an oversized high-vis jacket. I couldn't hear them laughing in their car, but I could guess they were, just from the small clues. Like the finger pointing at me, and them being doubled over in hysterical laughter.

My sister's pony is called Mr Toffee. Mr Waste of Money would be more accurate. This super-sized pet gets better shoes than me. If you look up the word 'pony' in the dictionary, it should say 'angry, pooing motorbike'. Why would any sane human want to sit on an animal that can go crazy and run off at any moment? They are huge beasts, yet will head for the hills at top speed at the mere sight of a packet of crisps. Sometimes they just decide to throw you up in the air and break your bones for the pure fun of it.

I could see Dad out the front of our house depooing his car. My sister was nowhere to be seen of course. Probably counting her new rosettes and making space for them on her bedroom wall. Dad's car is not a BMW like Artie's dad's. We had to sell our decent family car for a second-hand one to fund Mr Toffee's stable fees. So now we travel around in an estate car from the olden days all so Mr Toffee can sleep in luxurious five-star accommodation – with en suite hay. I'm talking wind-down car windows. It's the colour of sick. Dad says it's 'golden sunrise', but, trust me, the only way you'd ever see a sunrise this colour is if the world was ending and the sun was throwing up into the sea.

Whenever Dad picks me up from school, I ask him to park a few streets away so no one can see him. Often he will think it's 'hilarious' to wait for me right outside the school gates, playing nursery rhymes at full volume and yelling at me, 'Got your favourites on, Spike!' Dad's very funny. To himself.

I think he does all of this because his job is *sooooo* boring. He's the manager of the local supermarket, but he used to be cool once, a very long time ago. He was a drummer in a band and that's how Mum met him. Mum makes us all feel a little bit sick when she starts telling 'our story'.

'Your dad was in the coolest band in town; everyone was talking about them being the next big thing. One night after a show I invited myself backstage and we kissed.'

I've seen photos (no videos as they hadn't been invented back then; I think people drew on cave walls) and maybe it was a different time, but you don't see many famous bands these days with all the members wearing eyepatches.

'We were called the Pirates you see, son. That

was our gimmick. If you liked a girl in the crowd, you lifted up your eyepatch, like I did when I spotted your mum,' Dad would confide, creepily.

It turns out they weren't the next big thing or even the one after that. Sadly, the Pirates broke up on the cusp of being signed to a major record label at the age of just eighteen. Mum says we aren't to ask Dad about what split the band up ('it could upset him'). But I heard them talking about it late one night. They'd been at a party and Dad had bumped into the Pirates' former lead singer, Tom Dibble, who now runs a tanning salon in town. It was the first time I'd ever heard my dad swear. After playing Count the Swear Words (seventeen, including one I didn't understand; Holly did when I told her – she said her mum called her dad it once when he shrank her favourite jumper), I finally found out what broke up the band.

It would appear that Tom, the Pirate singer,

took the rock-and-roll behaviour too far. Despite having a girlfriend, he thought it would be no problem to have a spare one. The only problem was that the spare one turned out to be my Aunt Charlotte. Dad's sister. When she discovered she was the bonus girlfriend, she came home in tears and Dad had a fight with his Pirate bandmate in the middle of a show. Oh, wouldn't you have wanted to see that? Two pirates fighting live on stage – walk the plank, Tom! As the other pirates tried to break up the fight, the microphone got smashed into Pirate Tom's teeth. A tooth was knocked out and into the drink of an audience member.

Tom really *did* look like a pirate after that, it would seem.

Despite much dental work, the Pirates had ended up with a lead singer with a slight but very audible whistle when he sang. The record deal never happened and they split up a few weeks later. Sometimes Dad is all fun and laughter until certain songs come on the radio and it will take him to his dark Pirate times. Then he starts staring madly into the distance, mumbling to himself the words of the band's biggest hit, 'Pirate Party in My Pants'.

'Pirate . . . party . . . pirate p-p-p-p-PARTY.'

Now Dad looked up from cleaning pony poo off the wing mirror of the old-mobile.

'You're back early. Everything all right, Spike?' he asked, unaware that the information I was about to give him was going to change our lives forever.

'Not great,' I said. 'I got fired from hospital radio.'

Dad put his serious face on. Frowning and everything.

'Sorry, son,' he said. He stretched his back. 'That must have been awful for you.'

'Yeah.'

'Well,' he said, 'life sometimes isn't very fair. But I'm telling you now, if you really want anything, there will always be setbacks along the way. What's important is how you handle them. No one gets anywhere without struggling.' Dad looked at me, seriously. 'Every day I wonder what could have been with the band. If we'd worked things out better, or if I'd taken up the offer to join the Dead Giraffes . . .'

After The Pirates broke up, Dad was offered a drumming spot in another band, the Dead Giraffes. However, disillusioned with fame and fortune, he joined the trainee management scheme at the supermarket he now runs. He's done well.

Not as well as the Dead Giraffes though, who went on to have five number-one hits in thirty different countries.

'But . . . how do I keep going?' I asked, bringing him back from one of the thousand-yard stares that goes with him reminiscing about his drumming glory days.

'Simple. Get back on the horse.'

'The horse?'

'I mean, find another show,' said Dad. 'Get back on the radio somehow.'

'Easier said than done,' I pointed out. 'Although Holly wants to make the school finally start its own radio station . . .'

'That's the spirit!' said Dad. 'Or just do it yourself. You watch all those kids with online shows, but it's not just videos. There are online radio stations too, Spike, playing much better music than all that pop rubbish you hear now. I love this one called New Music Is All Rubbish. It's a brave new world out there on the interweb. Why don't you launch your own one? Do the *Spike Show*.' Dad's serious face changed into his excited one. Which is maybe scarier.

'Where from? I don't have a studio,' I replied.

He obviously hadn't thought it through. What my dad said next will go down in history as the dumbest idea ever.

'Do your show from the shed.'

An innocent suggestion from a dad trying to help out his desperate loser son.

But those fateful words started this whole mess.

CHAPTER 5

Loser FM

'WHAT? The shed! The buried jungle temple? Where a whole community of spiders with fangs and rats live? Are you kidding me, Dad?' I yelled.

'Spike! You're missing the bigger picture,' said Dad, warming to his idea now. 'You'd be your own boss: no one to fire you or tell you what to do. We'd have to keep it a secret from your mum or she'd never allow it. Your mate Holly can get it up and running, I'm sure. Ask Mr Taggart, the

AV Club teacher, for some help. I'll help you too. Don't do what I did and walk away from your dream. Chase it.'

'Dad, have you ever heard of anyone doing a radio show from a shed? It's pathetic. Look, it's OK, Dad. Keep your shed. It's got all your paint pots and the lawnmower in and it's covered in thorns and weeds. I'm going to chill out in my bedroom.' I left him to his car-cleaning, my head low and dejected. I dragged myself upstairs.

As I climbed the stairs, I bumped into my sister, who'd been listening to everything.

Her eyes narrowed as she said, 'Oh dear. Little brother's been sacked and is now launching Loser FM live from the shed?'

Amber was loving this. Remember: her weekend highlight would've been sitting on Mr Toffee's back, being carried around a field, praying the beast didn't launch her into the air just for a laugh.

'Not now,' I sighed, and tried to get past.

But Amber blocked the way. She was dressed in her riding gear and stank of manure and attitude. A fresh red rosette the size of her face was pinned to her.

'Maybe you could do the show from the toilet? Perfect for your material,' she kindly suggested.

'Ha ha,' I said. I was too tired to think of a comeback.

Her smile widened. 'Oh, and I couldn't help but notice you've doodled Katherine Hamilton's name all over your desk.'

'YOU'VE BEEN SNOOPING IN MY ROOM!' I yelled.

'It's so sweet,' she replied. 'The first flush of romance . . .'

'I hate you,' I said. I could feel – with horrified embarrassment – that I was about to cry. I took a deep breath.

Suddenly, Amber's face softened. 'I don't know

why you like her so much anyway,' she said. 'She's horrible. She is *not* the girl you were friends with in primary school.'

I was confused. Was Amber being nice now, caring about me?

I wasn't confused for long.

'Anyway, so long, loser,' she said. And with that she walked off.

As I flopped on to my bed, I heard a key in the front door. My dog Sherlock ran under my bed as if he knew a storm was coming.

Mum was back.

I heard her and Dad talking briefly, and the word 'sacked' sounded loud and clear. Then it went quiet. Too quiet. Eerily quiet. My mum swore. Very loudly.

'The loser! I'll stick his headphones . . .'

Technically it's impossible to do what she suggested to Barry Dingle – the Beyerdynamic headphones are very big – but I'd have liked to have seen her try. Sherlock pushed himself even further under the bed.

Then footsteps. Mum was coming up the stairs. No, running up the stairs. Two or three at a time. The whole house was shaking. Carol Hughes had been given bad news and things were about to go NUCLEAR.

'WHERE is my poor angel?' Mum asked before she was even in the room.

Now she was here, almost ripping my bedroom door off its hinges. The first thing I noticed was the red, angry face. You could've seen it on Google

Earth. My mum isn't tall and not really short either, but she has the power of ten men, according to my dad.

'Tell me what that SLAP-HEADED

coward did! Tell me everything!' Mum yelled as she stood in my bedroom, hands on her hips, her tracksuit soaked in sweat from her Zumba class.

'Well . . . um . . . he fired me.'

'Why?' asked Mum.

'Apparently no one was listening.'

Mum stared out of the window and started chewing her bottom lip. This wasn't good. This meant she was hatching a plan.

'RIGHT! It's clear to me that what you need now is a new hobby. It's not going to do any good moping around here, Spike. You have to make some new friends,' Mum declared.

'I already have friends and don't want to join any more clubs, Mum,' I pleaded.

In the vain hope of moving me up the school popularity rankings, my mum had made me join various clubs. Gymnastics, scuba-diving and Air Cadets. I hated them all.

My gymnastics career ended with me crashing

into some parents who had the misfortune to be sitting near my high beam. Scuba-diving ended when I dropped an air tank on to the instructor's foot, breaking not one but several bones. He swore and said a good selection of the words my dad said that night when I learned the story about Tom, the Pirates' lead singer.

Air Cadets ended after the first meeting at the community centre when Squadron Leader Gary told Mum that many of his cadets went on to join the air force and fly fighter jets.

'No son of mine is sitting in a rocket with wings, firing bombs at dangerous people, plus his ears play up just flying on holiday to Spain,' were my mum's final words.

Now, though, her mind was made up and resistance was futile.

'Nonsense,' she said. 'Sensei Terry has a spare place in his karate class. I'm calling him now to sign you up.'

'Oh, please don't—'

'My mind is made up, Spike. I'm only doing what's best for you,' she said. This was one of my mum's classic catchphrases. Along with:

- 'It could kill you stone-cold dead in seconds': applied to almost anything and everything, from food that is seven minutes past its sell-by date to swimming within an hour of eating a 'heavy meal'.

- 'What would people say?': again, Mum is constantly worried about what neighbours and friends might say, like when my sister Amber said she wanted to get her ears pierced. This got a record high score of three Mum catchphrases within less than three seconds. 'You want YOUR EARS PIERCED, AMBER? No way, madam. A dirty, infected needle could kill you stone-cold dead in seconds; what would people say? I'm only doing what's best for you.'

I could only think of one way of getting out of this. Use my mum's worry that danger lies round every corner. I think she gets it from working at the hospital.

'Isn't karate a bit . . . dangerous?' I said, mock-innocently.

But she was wise to me. 'Sensei Terry is all about avoiding violence,' she said. 'He'll teach you to protect yourself. From murderers and that. Just what you need.'

'I don't need protecting from murderers.'

'You never know,' she said. 'Anyway, Holly goes, doesn't she? So you'll have a friend there. It'll be fun.'

'Fun'. Now there's a word I'd love to ban. 'Fun' is a word parents use to describe something that's rubbish or boring to try to kid you it isn't.

No, karate wouldn't be fun. It would be yet another painful reminder that sport and me hate each other.

CHAPTER 6

Mae GERi !

These are my two favourite things to do at school:

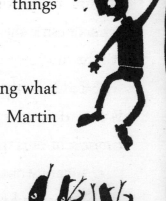

1. Closing my eyes and imagining what it would be like to throw Martin Harris into a pit of snakes.

   The snakes won't have eaten for a year and will have been

told that Martin killed their Snake Dad. Martin Harris is officially my School Enemy Number One. Most of us have a nemesis. Someone who was put on this planet to make your life a misery. You've done nothing to them, and leave them alone, but they somehow find you and it's as if you've stolen everything they've ever owned. Dad tells me you also get them when you're a grown-up. The supermarket area manager is his. Though I doubt his nemesis once tried to shove his head down the toilet.

Martin Harris is Mr Perfect. Captain of the school football, rugby, cricket and swim teams. He's also the son of the headmaster, Mr Harris, who I think created Martin in the science lab. Worse than him constantly trying to ruin my life at school is the fact that Katherine Hamilton (the girl I want to marry) thinks he's great. This is only because she hasn't really spent much time with me since primary school, when we used to be friends and play at each other's houses.

2. Going home.

'Your school years are the best years of your life, son.'

My dad told me this once, just before I stepped out of his car and into a steaming pile of dog poo, right outside the school gates.

My school is St Brenda's. Named after one of the lesser-known saints, 'Brenda', who, judging from this place, must be the patron saint of boring kids to death. I walk around like I'm invisible. Sure, I've got my gang of Artie and Holly, but at St Brenda's, if you aren't great at sport, you're about as cool as a boy caught dancing with his mum at the school disco.

All week, I'd been getting used to living in a

world of being sacked. On the TV news I'd seen a football manager being fired, and now I felt an instant bond with him. Luckily for me, *my* sacking hadn't involved fans waving big banners saying 'SACK THE CLOWN' and 'YOU SUCK'.

Normally, I looked forward to the weekend and to that one hour on a Saturday when I was king of the hospital radio airwaves. Now all that was waiting for me at the end of the week was the dreaded karate lesson. I had been thinking about Dad's idea of doing my own show, but two things kept coming up:

1. The sadness of doing it from my dad's garden shed.
2. Mum never letting it happen due to various worries, like me being mauled by a wandering bear or struck by lightning.

But the reality was that it was possibly the

only way I had of doing radio again. Unless the school did launch its own station, in which case I'd be the only one for the job. But I didn't share Holly's optimism about that. Headmaster Harris had been promising us a radio station for *ages*.

Right now, though, I didn't have the energy to worry about getting back on the radio, because I was heading to my first ever karate lesson. After much initial moaning at Mum's decision to make me go, I had to admit I was now a bit excited. This was down to two things.

Firstly, Holly had told me that Katherine Hamilton (the girl I was going to marry) would be there. This was the perfect opportunity to finally impress her.

Secondly, I LOVE fight scenes and action movies. I've often thought I could easily be a stuntman if prime-time radio doesn't happen for me. Everyone should have a back-up plan: it's just smart thinking. I have an Iron Man poster on my bedroom wall. I like to look at it and imagine being the stand-in who does all Robert Downey Jr's amazing stunts.

One evening, I made the mistake of telling Mum about my dreams of Hollywood stardom. She looked at the poster and all she said was, 'Well, you need to get your maths grades up.' As a lifelong member of the bottom set in maths, I knew that would be hard work. And, anyway, why would a stuntman need pie charts and fractions?

Brave though Iron Man is, he never has to face my personal hell of the boys' changing room. Sure, it's a fun place if you are one of the boys who look like Olympic athletes, with the early signs of hairs on your chest. But for the rest of us it's a nightmare, nervously trying to take our clothes off without the other, bigger apes seeing you.

While getting ready for the karate lesson, there was an early sign this was not going to go to plan when Martin Harris strutted in, chewing gum.

Soon as he saw me, he shouted over, 'Girls' changing room is over there, Spike!' and his mutant ape mates all laughed.

After some warm-up star jumps, the karate class was ordered to line up. Sensei Terry walked out with his hands proudly resting on his black belt. *Cooool!* Like a cowboy with his belt and holsters, except this was a gym hall in a community centre, not the Wild West.

He bowed.

'Welcome, Spike,' he said. 'To our class.'

'Um, thanks, Terry.'

'Call me Sensei!' he said sternly. Almost barking at me.

You might remember that Sensei Terry was also our local Neighbourhood Watch leader and postman. (Dad had asked me to check with Sensei Terry after the class about a parcel he was waiting for.)

Sensei Terry proceeded to demonstrate a front

kick. Or, as he described it, in his unique Japanese accent, 'Mae Geri . . . MAE GERI.'

Hearing the Japanese word for this technique, I felt suddenly excited again, at the prospect of this ancient art being passed on from Master (Terry the postman) to promising young protégé (me). All in a sports hall that stank of cheesy feet, and that we had to vacate by 5pm, as that was when my mum's Zumba class started.

I could do this. Sensei Terry called out for a volunteer. I shot my hand up. This was my moment to impress Katherine Hamilton (the girl I wanted to marry).

He picked me. Sensei Terry *knew* there was something about me. This promising newcomer who showed raw potential. Maybe just something in the way I had swaggered into the community hall. As if I belonged there. The Master had finally found his apprentice. Sadly, just walking out to the front of the class wasn't easy due to my karate outfit.

About that. I'd asked my mum for a new karate uniform to wear to my first lesson. Dad agreed and looked online at one made in Japan, the home of karate.

'This is the one, Spike,' he said, 'as worn by three-time World Champion Chuck Chuckerson.' My dream of owning such a sacred garment was only one Dad click away. Sadly, this moment was to last less than 0.09 seconds as Mum stopped Dad mid-sentence to remind him that there was already a 'perfectly good' karate uniform in the house. My big sister's.

'YOU'VE GOT TO BE KIDDING ME, MUM!' I pleaded.

'If you actually stick to this class, then your dad will get you a new one,' she said.

Dad may be many things, but in this house the real Sensei is Mum – with a black belt in cheapness. If Dad died, I think – rather than pay for a proper wooden coffin – she'd just put him in a shoebox and bury him in the garden, like we did my sister's hamster, Mr Whiskers.

This karate outfit, or 'gi' as I later learned it was called from Terry the samurai postman, hardly fitted as it had shrunk after Dad put it in the tumble dryer for too long. It would have been uncomfortable on a small dog, let alone an eleven-year-old like me, who was about to become a highly trained fighting machine.

'Spike here will show us how easy it is, won't you?' said Sensei Terry.

'Yeah, Terry,' I replied.

'It's *Sensei!*' the samurai postman screamed back, his words almost punching the air.

'Yes – sorry, Sensei,' I replied meekly.

'OK, so, Mae Geri front kick NOW!'

We were in a 'front stance'. Which meant left foot forward and right leg behind. I was coiled like a cobra, ready to strike. As my rear leg came up like the mighty Sensei Terry had just demonstrated, I fired my foot into an imaginary attacker's stomach (*not really imaginary – Martin's*), and ... there was a tremendous tearing noise.

Suddenly, I could feel fresh air around my backside. This wasn't going to be my moment to impress Katherine Hamilton or become a Hollywood stuntman.

My karate trousers had split.

To be precise – my sister's karate trousers had split.

In front of the whole class. But, worse, in front of Katherine Hamilton (the girl I wanted to marry).

CHAPTER 7

Chess club nightmares

Leading the laughing and pointing at what my split karate trousers had revealed was, of course, School Enemy Number One, Martin Harris. The tear had revealed my underpants. They were Iron Man underpants.

Yeah, I know, *Iron Man underpants*. Please don't judge me. My mum got them when I was younger and they were the only clean ones to wear that day.

It was obvious I could never, ever go back. I

had brought shame on this ancient art form and I'm pretty sure the samurai code didn't allow its warriors to wear their big sisters' clothes. The laughing, the pointing, the Iron Man underpants: this would now become yet another nightmare I would relive forever.

For days afterwards, as I walked the school corridors, I could see people looking at me, sniggering, trying to hide their laughter, and hear the yells of, '*Hey, look, IT'S IRON MAN!*'

Or worse, '*He wears his SISTER'S CLOTHES!*'

Yeah, yeah. Laugh it up! Then GET INTO THE PIT OF SNAKES, MARTY!

My stuntman career was over before it had even begun.

That evening, I was hit with another MMB (Mum Mind Bomb). As she turned out my bedroom light, she chillingly said, '*Don't worry, there's always the Chess Club.*'

As I slept, I had terrible nightmares of Katherine Hamilton in a wedding dress, walking down the aisle with a man in my clothes – except it was Martin Harris. I wasn't going to be marrying Katherine. Instead, I was playing chess with the vicar at the back of the church.

No! I thought when I woke up, sweating coldly from the nightmare. *Not Chess Club.* This had to stop, and only one thing could halt Mum on a mission.

I've got to get back on the radio.

There was nothing else for it: I was going to have to try out Dad's idea, and start broadcasting from the garden shed.

There was one big Mum-sized problem with that plan, though, as I will explain in the next chapter, if you're still reading this horror story.

CHAPTER 8

the next chapter

Another thing I like to think about at school, other than going home and snake pits and School Enemy Number One, Martin Harris, is sacking my parents.

OK, maybe that's a bit harsh, but wouldn't it be amazing if at least we actually ran our own parents' evenings? Instead of them sitting down for a cosy chat with our teachers about our efforts, we would sit down with our parents and 'review' how *they* have performed over the year.

Of course, there wouldn't be in-depth analysis about their progress in maths, English or science. The subjects up for discussion at this parents' evening would be a little bit more interesting.

This would be my dad's report.

Dad's Report

Subject: Meltdowns

In science one day, Mr Boron told us about something called DNA. He said it was 'the code of life'. Every human has genes that make up who we are. I think in my dad's DNA there must be a MELTDOWN gene. He can be all calm for weeks on end, then all of a sudden, with no warning, something very small will make him explode – like a volcano in slippers.

Take last week, when he couldn't find the

TV remote control. A weird vein came up on his neck and started throbbing. It looked like an angry worm. Mum told him helpfully to 'calm down', which made the worm double in size. He went off like a dad firework.

'REMOTE . . . MISSING . . . WHY CAN'T ANYONE JUST PUT IT WHERE IT SHOULD BE? ON THE COFFEE TABLE . . . I AM CALM, CAROL!'

At this point, Mum breezed in, reached down the back of the couch and instantly found it. Dad was still mumbling about it an hour later, threatening to put a chain on the remote control, like they do with pens in the bank.

Mark: *F. Fail. Must try harder, Dad.*

Subject: Gifts

Dad is pretty good at choosing Christmas and birthday presents. Better than Mum, who will always insist on trying to find a cheaper version of the gift I want. Last Christmas, when I asked for a pair of Nike trainers, my dad said, 'Yes, son, sure – just ask Father Christmas nicely.'

Only nanoseconds later, Mum gave him what Dad calls the 'death stare'. This guaranteed I ended up with trainers from the market that would have made Santa's elves cry to look at.

Mark: *F. Good effort, Dad. Next time just ignore Mum. Like a real pair of Nike's, Just Do It, Dad.*

Subject: Odour

You do not want to go into a toilet after my dad has been in there for a long visit. My dad's favourite room in the house seems to be the toilet. He likes to keep a wide selection of books and newspapers in there. It's like a very smelly library.

Mark *F: Fail. Use an air freshener.*

As for Mum, let me show you her end-of-year report.

Mum's Report

Subject: Talking

My mum really likes to talk. All the time. On phone calls, in the school playground, to strangers in the street, to a man walking his dog, to neighbours and of course to the postman (Sensei Terry). In my view, a large percentage of these people don't actually want to talk to her. (With the possible exception of Sensei Terry, who shares her obsession with the comings and goings on the street.) This makes no difference to my mum. She just carries on regardless.

The phone is her main weapon of choice. Dad says we should get her a call-centre headset for Christmas, so she can make multiple calls simultaneously. It seems to Dad and me that these calls are mainly to school mums she spoke to only minutes ago in the playground, making sure they understand EXACTLY what she wants them to do. Follow her orders.

She is at her worst when we go on holiday. Mum will strike up a conversation with any available family and then for the rest of the trip we are forced to eat dinner with them every single night. Without fail, she always manages to pick a really boring and annoying family that we all end up hating (even Mum). We then have to give false contact details when we say goodbye in the hotel lobby in case they ever decide to visit or attempt to contact us again.

Mark: *F. Fail. (Can't keep quiet for more than 3.7 minutes.)*

Subject: Embarrassing Me

Mum embarrasses me on a daily basis. I've started to think she must be filming a hidden-camera TV show called *Ruin Your Son's Life*. Last week, at the school gates, she shouted to me in front of the whole school, 'Don't forget to rub the cream into your eczema.'

Then there was the cinema humiliation. I went to watch *Jurassic World* with some friends, but I didn't tell her as she'd have said no. Somehow she found out, though, from her network of spies (other mums, terrified of her) and she stomped into the cinema and called out my name. My world suddenly became more terrifying than the sight of a pterodactyl ripping a man's head off. At first my friends all laughed, then even they went quiet as she came closer.

'Spike, come with me RIGHT NOW. You know you'll have nightmares, like you did when you watched Harry Potter and thought your dad was Voldemort.'

That night I did have a nightmare. That a dinosaur got into our house and ate my mum. That wasn't the nightmare bit. It was that the dinosaur spat her back out.

Mark: *F. Fail. But really an A because she's just so good at it.*

Subject: Snooping
(This is the important one so really slow down and read this properly.)

My mum likes to spy on people. Actually, that's a bit inaccurate: she LOVES to spy on people. I know for a fact that she searches my room almost every day. It's like being under constant surveillance from an overly suspicious prison guard. Is she searching for hidden digging tools that she thinks I'm planning to use to tunnel out and escape?

And, as I've said, nothing goes on in our street without my mum knowing about it. If something unplanned does occur, she'll hide behind the net curtains in the front room to get a better view. We then hear these frontline reports:

'Who is that outside Number 52 in the removal van . . . ? And Number 48 . . . Have they split up? Never trusted him, eyes too close together.'

Then she will be straight on the phone to her network of spies.

'Hi, it's Carol . . . you seen what the Meachers have outside their house right now? Did you know anything about this? No? Me neither. What do you think it's about? *Blah-blah-blah-de-blah blah-blah.'*

She'd make a great spy.

'The name's Bond, Carol Bond. Licence to pry.'

Mark: *A+*

Which leads me to the big problem with Dad's plan.

What was he thinking, believing that we could keep a radio show in the shed a secret from Carol 'the spy' Bond?

To my surprise, though, something happened the next day that changed everything.

Something I was *not* expecting.

CHAPTER 9

Merit Radio

'Spike, you're going to be back on the radio!' Holly said, excitedly.

News had spread around the school that there was going to be a special assembly and it was all about the launch of a new school radio station.

Hope was not lost! Dad's shed would thankfully not be required.

We had been asking Mr Harris for *ages and ages* about setting up a radio station. We'd even organised a petition that most of the school signed. I say most, as Martin Harris and his mutant apes didn't. It wasn't that they couldn't spell their own names, it was just that Martin snapped my pen in half when I gave it to him to use. None of this mattered now, though, as all our hard work in the AV Club seemed about to be finally recognised.

'You think they'll pick us to do it?' I said.

'Of course!' said Holly. 'We're the AV Club, aren't we? And you're the only one with actual presenting experience.'

I allowed myself a half-smile. She was right. We were surely the only candidates to run it. This was it. The dream was back on.

'Class, can you all please head to the main hall for the special assembly. Mr Harris has some very exciting news about . . . well, I don't want to ruin his surprise,' Miss Taylor, our form teacher, told the class.

The entire school walked in hushed silence to the main hall where all our assemblies and school plays were held. All the headmaster's assemblies began this way, with the walk of silence. Mr Harris would stand at the top of the steps that lead into the hall, watching us all file past, like a prison warden keeping an eye on the inmates.

'Surprised we don't have to wear handcuffs as well,' said Holly.

'Shh,' I replied. The last thing I wanted to do was upset my chances of getting a show on this new radio station.

St Brenda's school all sat in obedient silence. Mr Harris walked out, waited for a few seconds, then began talking. All of this was conducted in the manner of a world leader at a press conference announcing world peace, rather than a jumped-up teacher just speaking to eight hundred bored schoolkids. Well, 797 bored kids, since Artie, Holly and I were super-excited.

'Good morning!' Fish Face began. Did I mention that's what we call our beloved headmaster, Mr Harris? When he talks, it's like a big fish blowing bubbles, with his large puffy cheeks and massive bulging eyes.

'Some of you may be aware that there has been a campaign to get St Brenda's its very own radio station. Well, if there's one thing Mr Harris is known for, it's listening to his pupils,' said a grinning Fish Face. He's the only person I know who, when they grin, look totally terrifying. Like a shark smiling at you before it bites you in half. Except this is a shark covered in sausage-roll crumbs. Mr Harris *loves* jumbo sausage rolls.

Our great leader was still going on. 'I can announce to you all now that St Brenda's *will* be launching its very first radio station . . .'

Wild applause and cheers ran through the main hall. This was school history in the making. Fish Face was in his element, enjoying every moment. His gormless son was leading the applause. Clapping like a demented seal. Despite our grievances, it was very sporting of Martin to cheer this news as I'd thought he hated me. I guess people can change.

'Now, many of you will want to be part of this exciting new adventure. On the microphone, behind it, helping make the programmes. Today I would like to tell you who will be the voice of our station. Radio is one of the oldest mediums in the world. It is a friend to everyone. There is someone in this room who embodies all that radio is about, and is dedicated to continuing its legacy for the next generation. This person has a unique passion.' Mr Harris paused.

The entire school looked round at me, including Mr Taggart, our AV Club teacher, who gave me a reassuring wink. Holly, Artie and I couldn't contain ourselves. I was wide-eyed with excitement. Christmas Day was here right now.

'It wasn't easy arriving at this decision as there were several very worthwhile contenders, but the pupil who will be on air and launching Merit Radio will be. . . '

'*Get on with it, Fish Face,*' said Artie, a little too loudly.

'. . . MARTIN HARRIS.'

Wait.

What?

Who?

I must've misheard him. Not Martin. That just wouldn't happen.

'Yes, Martin Harris. Merit Radio will be celebrating all that's great and good about St Brenda's. Each lunchtime, pupils who have achieved high grades will have their names read out on the air, as I believe you disc jockeys say. Martin Harris may be my son, but he has, by quite a long shot, the highest number of merits in the school, so that's why he is the very best person to launch Merit Radio. No one can argue with that.'

Everything went very quiet and into slow motion. The first thing I noticed was Mr Taggart staring at Mr Harris, stunned. He got up and quietly walked out. He obviously hadn't been consulted on this decision. I thought I was going to be sick. Artie and Holly were speechless. Everyone looked round at me again, this time in a pitying way. Like driving past a car crash. Even my older sister looked over, concerned.

Martin Harris! A radio DJ! How? He lasted one AV Club, called us all nerds at the end of it and never came back. We silently shuffled out of the hall, and Artie and Holly guided me back to our classroom. My eyes were filling with tears. I couldn't cry, not in front of everyone. The final blow was seeing Katherine Hamilton (the girl I want to marry) rushing over to congratulate Martin Harris. That ape had only got his overdose of merits because he was the headmaster's son and all the teachers wanted to keep their jobs.

What even was 'Merit Radio'? Radio for school goody-two-shoeses and their high grades. They wouldn't even hear it; they'd be in the library, swotting up. That's not what radio should be about. Who wants to hear guff like that? A Fish Face is who.

It felt like my world had just been blown apart. I was back on the outside looking in. A spectator on the sidelines.

The hardest thing, what really hurt the most, was that all hope had gone.

That was until I got home and opened the mysterious gift-wrapped box that was waiting for me on my bed.

CHAPTER 10

The supermarket detective

A brand-new microphone.

A big silver one, like actual, proper DJs use, and a brand-new pair of headphones. That's what was in the mysterious gift-wrapped box on my bed. I was so confused. Who would do this and why? Not Mum, that's for sure. These weren't cheap pound-shop ones.

I didn't have to wait long for the answer. Attached to the microphone was a note in my dad's messy handwriting, saying, *'Meet me in the shed.'*

I followed the instructions and ran out to the bottom of the garden. Sherlock trotted excitedly alongside me; even *he* was curious to find out what was going on. I've often thought, *Wouldn't it be great if dogs could talk?*, but I think they could be really boring. Like that kid at school who clings on to you and wants to know what you're doing and where you're going all the time.

Dad's shed wasn't the easiest to find. It's not like we have a big garden or anything, but it's almost completely hidden under all the overgrown bushes, most of which are like barbed wire and cut you to ribbons if you try to get past them. To the rest of the family it's a no-go area. Which may have been Dad's plan, as he likes to disappear in there sometimes. There's a very high chance of you bleeding to death just trying to get in, and then you have to contend with what's behind the shed door. Giant rats, angry wasps and entire colonies of ants. It's like a horror movie: *The Little Shed of Horrors*. It even has its own weather system. Whatever the actual weather is outside, inside the Shed of Horrors it will somehow be the exact opposite. Hot outside? Polar bears will be shivering inside. Cold outside? Then you can guarantee the ants will be sunbathing.

SHED →

Mum has only ever ventured into the shed once, and came running straight out, screaming as if she'd encountered a fire-breathing dragon with a clown's face. She was convinced she'd seen a deadly scorpion, and called the pest-control man. Who found a spider.

Other humans would've been slightly embarrassed by this and apologised to the pest-control man for wasting his time – not my mum though. This was yet another chance to warn us about the danger that is everywhere.

'Well, it must've escaped then. I scared it away thankfully before it stung you, Spike. Trust me, I've seen in my hospital with my very own eyes the effects of a scorpion sting. I'm talking unable to go to the toilet ever again without several medical professionals helping you with machines. Machines, Spike!'

Have I told you yet that my mum has an unhealthy obsession with bowel functions? That's a posh way of saying a number two. Every single day I dread the question, 'Have you been to the toilet today yet?'

When I was younger, I had to fill out a daily poo chart she'd put up in my bedroom. I thought this was normal until Artie came round for the first time and asked what on earth the chart on my wall was with brown stickers and smiley faces. That was the very first moment I realised my mum wasn't like other mums. The poo chart. For the record, the poo chart doesn't exist any more, but I still get asked every day by the poo inspector, 'Have you been yet?' I reckon even when I'm, like, a grown-up and getting married Mum will run to the altar and whisper to me, 'Have you been yet?'

Today, though, this was a very different shed. The impenetrable wall of brambles was still in place, but what greeted me when I opened the rickety old door took my breath away. It was totally spotless inside. I could smell fresh paint. There had been a shed makeover. Colonies of exiled ants were fleeing the area angrily, looking for a new home. Dad was sitting there quietly having a cup of tea.

There were also some fold-out picnic chairs round the shaky-looking desk.

Dad carefully put his tea down on the desk/ wallpapering table, and the legs wobbled a bit.

'I heard what happened, what that idiot Mr Harris did,' Dad began.

'What, already?' I asked.

'Yes. Mr Taggart, your AV guy, came storming in at lunchtime today for his usual cheese and ham sandwich, crisps and industrial-strength coffee.' Dad listed these lunch items like a detective giving evidence. He not only knew all of his customers' names, he knew what they bought. *What my customers have in their weekly shop is as revealing about them as their fingerprints, son,'* the Supermarket Detective had said one day.

'Extra beer or wine? Maybe a party or a tough week. Nappies? A baby is coming. Extra salad? Someone is trying to lose weight. Probably poor Mrs Thomas – always looks like there are two people in her dress, bless her.'

'Normally, your Mr Taggart is a cheery guy,' continued Dad. 'But not today. I went over to say hello and he could hardly speak, son. Furious the man was, so I invited him into my office – you know the one, behind the deli counter.'

Dad calls this an 'office', but the sad reality is it's just a tiny desk in a storeroom that's more of a cupboard. The desk is the sort of thing you'd see in a kids' Wendy house. To get into this 'office' you have to navigate round the sausage rolls and pork pies. Hardly a high-flying executive suite, Dad.

'And . . . Mr Taggart told you about what Mr Harris did?' I asked.

'He did, son. Merit Radio! What a load of old tosh! The headmaster's son doing it all. What a total stitch-up! So I decided to tell him about my idea, about you doing your own internet show . . .'

Dad paused here. As if steadying himself.

'Spike, Mr Taggart LOVED the idea! He actually leapt out of his chair, knocking over some toilet rolls stacked in my executive office! He said he'd help in whatever way you needed.'

This surprised me. Mr Taggart would be willing to help me be a rival to Merit Radio? Couldn't he get into trouble for that?

'*Really?*' I said. 'He wants to help me set up . . . my own radio show?'

'Really, Spike. He believes in you, and I do too. The next bit is up to you. He can only do so much. No one you admire got where they are because it was easy. They never gave up. Do you really want this?'

I thought for a moment. 'Yes!'

'OK, Spike. You doing it alone?'

'NO! I need Artie and Holly to help. I can't do this ALONE.' I would need a support team and I couldn't think of anyone else. Maybe because there *wasn't* anyone else.

'Call them then. No time like the present.'

'*Now?*'

'Yes. Now. Get them to come here right away.'

'Um . . . OK,' I said.

'While you do that, I'll stick the kettle on and make another cuppa.'

We both went back to the house and I excitedly called Artie and Holly. I kept the conversation brief and just told them something amazing was happening round at mine. 'Get here as quick as you can – something amazing is happening,' I said.

Both wanted to know what, but I said what I'd heard characters say in movies when they are worried the phone's being bugged and someone is snooping on them.

'Not over the phone, it's not safe.'

Plus, I wouldn't put it past my mum to bug our own line.

CHAPTER 11

Like magic really

Artie and Holly were there as fast as their BMXs could carry them.

Once they were assembled in the front room, I brought them up to speed with Dad's plan and Mr Taggart.

'I can't do this without you two,' I said. 'I'm excited but . . . it's kind of scary too.'

'Scary why? You worried about your mum stopping you?' asked Holly.

'Well, not just that. More that no one will listen and I'll be an even bigger laughing stock than the kid who wore his sister's karate pants.'

'But you love radio, this is perfect for you,' said Artie.

'Yeah,' said Holly. 'It's all you've ever wanted to do. My dad always says, 'It's better to regret doing something you did than not do anything.' This is an opportunity, Spike. You've got to seize it.'

Holly was the most confident out of all of us. She was in the Army Cadets and stronger and more fearless than most of the boys. She joined after getting the idea from when I was briefly in the Air Cadets (remember?). Only, unlike me, she actually stuck at it.

Holly was Chief Telecommunications Officer. This meant she knew how the walkie-talkies worked when her 'unit' went on manoeuvres in the local woods. Don't get too excited: it meant a few out-of-breath kids with a compass shouting at each other and getting lost in an area the size of my bathroom. Apart from Holly.

I took them down to the shed and Dad walked behind us, casually sipping his tea. He nodded to us as if to say 'well done'.

As Artie and Holly entered the now-pristine shed, I could see they were taking it all in. We'd been friends long enough for them to know what a dump the place usually was.

Dad closed the shed door behind us.

'Welcome to your own radio station and show,' he said excitedly. His brown supermarket work tie wasn't hanging straight and was slung over one shoulder, giving us all another reminder that he was verging on insanity.

'I'm going to say something, and afterwards I want you all to think long and hard about it. Spike will have got you up to speed just now. You have two choices. To leave right away or stay.

If you stay, then the biggest adventure of your lives will begin right here.' You could have heard a pin drop in the shed. Sorry, studio. Even Sherlock was paying attention to this important briefing. Me, Artie and Holly exchanged looks.

'Look around you,' encouraged Dad. We did, our eyes scanning the freshly painted shed, my microphone and headphones. The startling image of my dad with his trousers pulled up a little too high.

'This is your rebel base, from which you can take on the world – well, Merit Radio anyway,' continued Dad.

Holly interrupted. 'This is really exciting, Mr Hughes, and forgive me for slowing this all down a bit, but how exactly are we, a bunch of kids, going to do it all? I mean, the technical side of it? It's very clean in here, but it's still . . . a shed.'

'Your Mr Taggart told me that you, Holly,

are the brains of this outfit, and will know how to do it. From what he told me, from my understanding . . . it's very simple and . . . I've got some sort of instructions here . . .'

This was going to be interesting. In my experience, explaining anything to do with computers and modern technology to my dad is like trying to tell a gibbering monkey how to land a plane.

Dad pulled what looked like a shopping list out of his pocket. On the other side was a series of diagrams apparently drawn by a caveman. Mr Taggart had given my dad a list of items we would need, and explained how to use them. He'd drawn pictures of it all. This information was now going to be passed on to us by my dad.

So this is how the Supermarket Professor broke down how to run an internet radio station to us.

You might want to make notes.

Dad Language	Correct Terminology
'Some black box with buttons'	A mixing desk
'Has those pushed into it'	Microphones
'It all goes into a lapthingy'	A laptop
'That speaks to her'	A Wi-Fi router
'That is beamed into your mates' cloth ears'	Broadcast to our audience
'Like magic really'	Modern science

I was actually impressed Dad had even understood that much.

Holly chimed in. 'I can do that, thank you, Mr Hughes. So the XLR cables, I'm guessing, must be standard 3.5mm, go into the mixer, then it's into the laptop and streamed to the world. We'll need better Wi-Fi and quicker streaming rates, Mr Hughes, though,' she reasoned as if discussing a route into town.

'Yes, yes, that's what I thought, Holly!' lied Dad.

In his mind, he still thinks magic pixies help download movies to our TV. He's not totally clueless though. His only punishment that really works on me and my sister is the threat of turning off the Wi-Fi.

My sister starts yelling, 'YOU CAN'T DO THAT! IT'S A BASIC HUMAN RIGHT TO HAVE WI-FI. THIS ISN'T CHINA, DAD, YOU KNOW!'

I just keep quiet as I know the router password anyway.

Dad pulled his trousers up even higher. This was a sign he meant business. If the house was on fire, the first thing my dad would do before leading us to safety would be to hike his pants up a bit higher. Anyway, now his trousers were at the required height he could continue his big speech.

'Leave aside the technical stuff for now. This show is serious business.' He fixed Artie and Holly with a trademark Dad stare. 'Spike's angry. He should be. He's been ignored and treated very unfairly. You're good friends if you join him in this, but have a think if it's really for you. And then think about the upsides too. This, right here, is where dreams can become reality.' He indicated the small shed. 'I know what that's like. Yeah, you may see me as some old guy who runs the town's most cost-effective supermarket, but not so long ago I was on the verge of the big time. I'm not sure if Spike has told you about my band, The Pirates?'

Of course I hadn't! Why would I?

'No? Really? Not a mention? Well, let me tell you, we were going to be the next big thing – record companies trying to sign us up. Stars on the verge of greatness. Well, it never happened. We broke up and then less talented bands took our spot. I was angry, invisible again, but do you know what the worst thing I did was?'

Dad was staring very intensely at the three of us. Sherlock was now dozing, the suspense obviously lost on him.

'Go and work in a supermarket?' offered Holly.

'No! The pension plan is fantastic, as is the health scheme. No, the worst thing was I DID NOTHING!' shouted Dad, banging his fist down to make the point. His DIY table really shook. Any more of this and my studio would be in pieces. *Easy, big guy.*

'Regret is a very strong thing,' he continued. 'It eats away at you. I beg you, don't get mad. Get even! Get funny. Use all this as a fire; don't let it burn inside you. Use it to fuel this . . . this new adventure. This here is a brand-new radio station. You are its stars. You run it. You are in charge.'

Dad dramatically indicated the microphone. That last bit really struck a chord with us. We would be in charge. Cool.

'It sounds fun,' said Artie. 'But I don't get it. I mean, why are you helping us, Mr Hughes?'

'Good question, Artie. Spike is my son, and I don't want to let him make the mistake I did, Artie, of giving up. I want him to follow his dream. And he can't do that alone. But at the end of the day the choice . . . is yours. Do you really want to do this? Start your own show right here? Do you want to show Mr Harris and that mutant kid of his how wrong they were? Do you want to try and give the kids of St Brenda's an alternative radio station? A real one. Artie, do you want to play your records to kids around the country? Holly, do you want to put all that cadet training into practice? In short: are you all in?'

And with those words he turned his back on us dramatically. There was silence in the shed.

CHAPTER 12

Shop-o-rama

'I'm in,' I said. 'I *need* to do this.' Part of me smiled as I said those words. Like I had awoken a deep desire sleeping within me.

'We *have* to do this,' Artie and Holly hissed behind my dad's turned back.

'I can do the music,' said Artie.

'I can do the tech stuff,' said Holly.

They were both grinning with the excitement of it all. However, I've no idea why they were whispering, given that, due to the size of the shed, Dad was standing less than a metre away.

Dad turned back to face us.

'So you're in?'

'Yes,' I said, and meant it.

'YES!' said Artie and Holly.

'Great!' announced Dad while rubbing his hands together, as if summoning some ancient spirits to help guide us. 'But keep your voices down. See, the only thing is . . .' He paused. 'Spike's mum can't know.'

'Actually . . .' I said. 'No one can know.'

'What?' said Artie. 'Why? What's the point of being radio stars if no one knows?'

'Think about it,' I said. 'Mr Harris won't like it, will he? I mean, we'll be competing with Merit Radio. And if anyone ever finds out about this radio show coming from this shed, or about how Mr Taggart advised us on how to make it, he could get in trouble. Plus, if Mum finds out, she'll just say no.'

'No sense in upsetting her just yet,' agreed Dad. 'Let's tell her soon, once we see how it all goes. She might . . . come round then.' He seemed to be trying to convince himself more than us.

'So we're agreed?' I said. 'We won't tell another soul?'

'Um, OK,' said Holly.

'I guess,' said Artie.

'OK,' said Dad. 'A secret club. A secret *radio* club. Your mum, Spike, and all your mums for that matter, are this town's biggest gossips. They are the best mums in the world, mind you, but if they find out you might as well broadcast it on Merit Radio.'

Dad made a good point there. We all nodded in agreement.

'When are we going to do the show?' I chipped in.

'Well, that took me and Mr Taggart a while. He's a smart one, believes in you all. He came up with the idea. The time of the AV Club will move a bit. Only you won't be there, you'll be here. Mr Taggart will cover and sign you in.'

My mind was racing, joining all the dots of how we could do it.

'We then sneak in here. By the back gate?'

'Smart thinking, son! You get that from your dad. So you'll need this, Spike . . .'

Dad threw me an old key.

'I didn't even know you had a back gate,' said Holly as I pocketed the rusty key. If the gate had escaped her military-trained eyes, then it *must* have been well hidden.

'Not many do, so it's perfect,' said Dad. 'You sneak in here and do the show, sneak back out and head home as if you've done another fun-filled AV Club. Tell your parents if anyone asks that you're all working on a special project for AV

Club. Smart, eh? Your mum normally works late on a Wednesday, Spike, so I'll keep guard in the house while you all work your magic in here.'

This was really happening now.

'Right, you lot carry on,' said Dad. 'You don't need me for this bit. You gotta work out what you're going to do – your first show is next Wednesday. Merit Radio starts Monday so you're giving them a few days' head start!'

'Mr Hughes,' said Holly. 'Just a small point. Erm . . . where are we going to get all the equipment from?'

'Yes, right, good question. You'll need these,' he said as he proudly handed us a load of egg boxes.

'What are these for?' I asked.

Holly had this one. 'Soundproofing! Good call, Mr H.'

'Exactly, Holly! See, you really are the brains here. And then, you go through this. Look for what you need.' Dad dropped on to the DIY table my mum's catalogue, SHOP-O-RAMA, which was around nine thousand pages thick and filled with cheap clothes, furniture and very basic electrical gear. 'Spike, I'm going to trust you with my credit card. Get the bare minimum. Don't go crazy.'

Dad left again, maybe off to make us a radio transmitter out of coat hangers.

We looked at each other, open-mouthed with excitement and a little bit scared. Don't all great adventures begin like that?

CHAPTER 13

The best shopping trip I ever went on

We flicked through the catalogue. Holly found the electrical page. Page. Not pages. Page. Which contained amazing items such as:

- A flimsy-looking set of walkie-talkies for kids that looked less reliable than yoghurt pots and string for chatting to your mate.
- A portable CD player called a 'Discman' for playing CDs on. Despite the fact that

the world stopped using CDs like that two hundred years ago.

- A very basic 'home computer', which was the size of a small family car. The couple advertising it were very old and laughing for no obvious reason while using the computer.

Looking at the catalogue was like being a time traveller and going back twenty years. Who even uses catalogues any more? Well, my mum. Old school.

'Right. We need a laptop for starters,' sighed Holly, closing the catalogue.

'I've got one,' said the person who of course *would* have a laptop. Artie, thanks to his rich parents. Probably powered by cream. He patted his giant backpack.

'Great,' said Holly. 'But we still need speakers, extra microphones, a Wi-Fi booster of some kind and, most important, a mixing desk.'

'Look, let's ditch the book of antique artefacts tat and really kit this place out as a radio studio,' I said.

'Car boot sale?' said Holly.

'Charity shop?' offered Artie.

'No! Let's look on eBay. You can get everything on there.'

'Hang on, Spike. Your dad never said anything about going on eBay!' said Artie.

'You saw how he wants us to crack on and make this happen. He gave me his credit card to get some gear. That's what we're doing. It'll save him money too – he'll thank me.'

'OK, open up your laptop, Artie, and let's go shopping,' said Holly.

And so we went on my favourite-ever shopping trip. Over the next hour we found what we were searching for. Our shopping list was looking good.

Speakers. From a nightclub shutting down on the other side of town called Crazy Larry's. Only downside being they had CRAZY LARRY'S in bright pink lettering down the side of them. Beggars can't be choosers.

Extra microphones. Got from a second-hand music shop. They looked very old. In the item description on eBay it said: 'Would suit rock band or museum.'

Wi-Fi extender. Listed as: 'Unwanted Christmas gift for elderly parents.' Was my dad selling it?

The thing that was proving tricky was the mixing desk. You probably won't know what this is, unless you're a member of your school Audio

Visual Club (AV Club), so I'd better explain a bit here. Imagine any studio where you see musicians and bands recording songs. There is always a big desk with loads of things called faders on it that slide up and down. Well, that's a mixing desk. Microphones, speakers and equipment all get plugged into it and you can adjust the volume of each. Turn the microphone down and the music up, for instance. It's the mother ship of the whole radio show. Lesson over.

Anyway. They were way out of my dad's budget, and on the only one we could afford on eBay, this kept happening.

We were in a furious bidding battle with a person going by the username *eatmycat58*.

Every time we made a bid, seconds later, Mr/Mrs/Miss *eatmycat58* would raise their bid by ONE POUND!

Who *was* this idiot? Martin Harris?

This went on for too long. We were being

held to ransom.

Time for me to take action.

'Right, enough with *eatmycat58*. Let's have a quiet word with Mr Taggart tomorrow at school to see if he can lend us a mixing desk.'

'Just so you understand, without one the show really isn't going to happen,' Holly stated.

'I get it,' I said.

That night I could hardly sleep with the excitement. As well as the worry about whether we'd obtain this last, crucial piece of equipment. Oh, and also the eBay parcels that would be arriving in Dad's name. I reminded myself to tell him about that. Soon.

CHAPTER 14

Shepherd's pie swamp

We had Mr Taggart for geography the next day. Like many teachers, he teaches two subjects. I always think that's funny. I mean our PE teacher also teaches French. It's a bit like a doctor running a sandwich shop in their spare time. At the end of the lesson – a very interesting one about tectonic plates and volcanoes – we hung back after class emptied out. Well, I did, as apparently, according to Artie and Holly, I'm his favourite.

'Everything OK, Spike?' Mr Taggart enquired.

'Well, yes. Erm . . .' I looked around to check no one could hear us. 'Thanks for helping us do our own show.'

Mr Taggart went over and closed the door, peering through the glass window to double-check no one could hear us.

'Carry on, Spike,' he said quietly. We were like two spies exchanging information behind enemy lines.

'We've managed to get all the stuff we need for the studio, apart from the mixing desk . . .'

'Right, well, you have been busy. Well done. How can I help? Oh, hang on, hang on! Oh no—' he said, realising what was coming next.

'We're being bidded out on eBay—'

'Outbid, Spike! OUTBID.' Mr Taggart was always a stickler for correct grammar. Even when involved in a highly illicit operation.

'Well, *eatmycat* is the problem, sir!'

'What on earth are you talking about, Spike?'

'*eatmycat58* is trying to OUTBID us,' I said.

'Ah, eBay. All right. Let me think.' Mr Taggart took a moment and his face frowned in deep concentration.

Think, Mr T, think!

'I've got it,' he said at last. 'There is a shiny brand-new mixing desk that just arrived yesterday. Top of the range. Incredible bit of kit—'

'Perfect! Thank you, Mr Taggart.'

'—that Mr Harris ordered for Merit Radio.'

I slumped into a chair.

'Don't worry. I do have one. It's old and basic, but all you need to do the job.'

'Thank you, thank you,' I said. The show would go on!

'Hang on, though, it's currently sitting by the recycling bins behind the school, as the cleaner took it there earlier ready for the bin men tomorrow. You'll need to find a way to go and retrieve it without anyone seeing you. Then get it out of here. Good luck. If you get caught then I will deny I told you any of this. Mr Harris won't like you doing your own show. Understood?'

'Yes, Mr Taggart.'

'Mr Harris is – how can I put this politely? – a very intimidating man, and I'm already in his bad books.'

'What for?'

'I parked in the wrong spot last week. No one knew there were "right" and "wrong" spots. But apparently there are. Anyway, he gave me a written warning, right there! Used a napkin to write a makeshift parking ticket on. He also threatened to take away my parking permit. Said he saw me as a future deputy head here and was disappointed in me, but would like to see me show him I'm still the right man for the job. That's a nice pay rise for me. Mrs Taggart could finally book that cruise she's always wanted. So that's why this all has to be under, way under, the radar. For the sake of my job here, and Mrs Taggart's cruise, and my parking spot.'

'Understood. Under the radar.'

'Good lad, now run along.'

'HOW ON EARTH ARE WE GOING TO DO THIS?' cried Artie, after I explained our new mission.

'It's simple. I have a plan.'

I relayed my cunning idea to them. They took some convincing, but this was the final item on our list, the only remaining thing we needed to make our own show happen, and we were so close. I texted my dad at work and told him to pick me up from near the school gates at 4pm, and have the engine running. He replied:

> If you're robbing a bank, can you get me £20,000? See you at 4.

At exactly 3.55pm, minutes before school ended, I pulled the fire alarm.

As you can imagine, teachers sprang into action.

'We all know what to do: leave in single file and follow me to the top playing field. SILENTLY AND CALMLY. Leave all bags here . . . GO . . . GO . . . GO,' ordered our science teacher, Mr Boron. (Also our head of drama. Two jobs.)

I did leave. Not, as instructed, to the top field – but in the opposite direction to find the back alley behind the school where the bins are. It takes quite a while to evacuate eight hundred kids: about the same time as it takes to find an old bit of radio equipment beside a bin.

Only the mixing desk wasn't by the recycling.

I couldn't see it anywhere. There *was* a big metallic bin with a big black lid I struggled to push open. Out came a terrible smell and hundreds of flies. I was really up against the clock.

I didn't have long until they realised it was a false alarm.

'Urggh!' I said as quietly as I could.

I held my nose and peered inside. Oh no. The cleaner had dumped the mixing desk in the bin along with all of lunchtime's leftover scraps.

I couldn't reach in and get it. There was a swamp of cold shepherd's pie and peas all around it.

But I *had* to. What was happening to me? Did I really want my own radio show this badly?

Apparently, I did.

I tried to reach in, but couldn't get to the mixing desk. I leant in even further as I stood on my tiptoes. Then something awful happened. Something that will give me nightmares FOREVER.

I fell in.

I leaned too far and lost my balance, and to anyone observing it must have looked like the bin swallowed me. Just my feet were sticking out of the top.

Then, from deep inside the bin, I heard the fire alarm stop.

They had discovered it was a false alarm.

My time was almost up. I had to get a move on. But I was head first in food leftovers and trying not to be sick. I didn't even have time to panic – I just reached for the mixing desk, smeared in mashed potato and carrots.

I peered out of the bin, breathing in gulps of beautiful fresh air. I was aware I was covered in leftover food. It would have to act as camouflage.

Now to get out of the swamp.

I swung one leg over, then the other, and landed on the ground with a soggy thud. I ran to the gate at the bottom of the school – the one hardly anyone ever uses. The one where I had told Dad to be waiting.

I made it out of the school gates, struggling to run with the soggy weight of the prized possession, heading to my getaway driver.

I will now tell you what my dad said he saw as he went over what happened in my bedroom at bedtime.

'I heard some yelling, looked in my rear-view mirror and got a fright. A strange-looking beast with a wild look in his eyes was running at me, carrying a box. It looked like he'd fallen into a vat of shepherd's pie. Then I saw it was you, and you flung the car door open and threw the machine smeared with cold mash and carrots in, while screaming, "GO, GO, GO!"'

We laughed quietly, and my eyes went to the now-clean mixing desk hidden under a blanket in the corner of my bedroom.

We were good to go. It was time to get ready.

How to start your own radio show in your dad's shed

MY HANDY STEP-BY-STEP GUIDE

In a history lesson at school one day, we were learning about the Second World War and how soldiers would carry letters to be opened by their family if anything happened to them.

Like a soldier, I thought I should put something down on paper about how we got the secret radio show ready to broadcast to the world, just in case

I was captured alongside my co-conspirators, Artie, Holly, Dad and Mr Taggart. (I don't think they have prisons for dogs. If they do exist, I hope it's clear that Sherlock didn't know what was going on and his fellow dogs on the jury find him innocent.)

If I do ever get in, like, serious trouble, I really hope the papers and TV news DO NOT USE my recent school photo. A tooth had just fallen out and my fake smile made me look like I was possessed by the devil.

ATTENTION, ALL MEDIA: YOU DO NOT HAVE MY PERMISSION TO USE THAT PHOTO.

STEP 1:

HIRE YOUR RADIO TEAM

TOP TIP: USE YOUR FRIENDS SO YOU DON'T HAVE TO PAY THEM

I offered Artie the role of head of music (in charge of just himself), which he accepted on one condition: that we would only play vinyl (those black plastic discs I mentioned). Oh, great. Thanks, Artie, why not make everything even harder?

This would mean somehow getting hold of a 'turntable' to play them on. He also wanted complete control of the music. I gave him that, though, as I didn't really care. I just wanted to do the show. Artie wants to work in the music industry one day and he saw this as his first break. It was a win-win, as I've heard Dad say.

Artie was also going to be my sidekick.

My favourite radio show is the breakfast show on Kool FM. The host is Howard 'Howie' Wright, and he's brilliant. Unlike other radio DJs, he's actually funny sometimes. He has a sidekick, Slim Jim (who is actually a chubby man), and it's often the chat between the two of them that makes the show as funny as it is. I needed a sidekick too. Artie always makes me laugh so he got the job.

So, by hiring Artie, I was hiring two people really: my head of music and my sidekick. He was like a Swiss army knife with all his uses.

I will detail shortly how we got hold of the turntable thing for the vinyl records. For you, it will be way easier. You won't have my antique-loving head of music. You could play music from your phone, or not play any music at all. Remember, it's your show.

Now every radio show needs a producer to make everything happen and to keep things in order. There was no one I knew better suited to that job than Holly. Lover of making lists and being super-organised, she would be perfect. Holly's experience on the battlefront of our local woods in her role as Chief Telecommunications Officer would be invaluable. However, I knew it was the covert nature of this adventure that really appealed to her, because Holly wants to work for a *'secret government department as a spy'.*

This was going to be a great opportunity for her to test her abilities to the max!

Holly leapt at the chance. 'I'll need total control over the mission, and I will provide codewords for us to use when discussing this project in the field,' she said.

'Field? Why will we be in a field?' I asked.

'Hmm. Sorry, "field" is what we call the real world.'

Right.

More importantly, she was the only one who

really knew how all the equipment worked. We were the perfect team.

Holly sat us all down and looked at her list.

'First things first. We need a name for the show, Spike,' she said.

This leads me to . . .

STEP 2:
NAME YOUR SHOW

TOP TIP: PICK A NAME THAT IS MEMORABLE AND ISN'T AS BORING AS 'MERIT RADIO' – I MEAN EVEN 'BLAH-BLAH-BLAH RADIO' WOULD'VE BEEN A BETTER NAME

I'll stop with the caps lock now.

This was really hard, coming up with a name for the show. Our shortlist was in fact far from short and kept getting longer.

- *The Midweek Freak Show*: because the show was going to be on a Wednesday night. Hardly genius.

- *Death to Fish Face*: we agreed that while this was very funny, it could be seen as a bit, you know, mean. The death bit in particular.

- *The Funky Monkeys*: Artie's idea – Holly and I said it made us feel physically sick it sucked so bad.

- *The Radio Rejects*: true, but it's not a very cool name, is it?

- *Dinner Ladies' Delight*

- *The Dog Ate My Homework*: can you tell we were getting tired and bored?

In the end, it was Artie who solved the problem.

'It's just a show in a shed that's secret,' Artie sighed.

'Yes, well done, Artie, thanks for that, Captain Obvious,' snapped Holly.

'No, he's GOT IT . . . THE *SECRET SHED SHOW*!' I shouted.

'YES!' the team agreed. High fives were exchanged.

'I also want a name,' I said.

'What do you mean? What's wrong with Spike Hughes?' asked Holly.

'No, no, no. This needs to all be secret, remember? I need a different name. If Mum finds out about all this, she'll put a stop to it – you heard my dad.'

'I know . . .' said Artie. 'But this is our chance to get noticed, to do something cool for once. Why hide like we always do?'

I paused.

'OK,' I admitted. 'I'm scared no one will tune in and, even if they do, what if I suck? I can't handle any more mickey-taking. I don't want yet another opportunity to fail at something. Spike Hughes is a nobody at school, and he will be a nobody on the radio.'

Artie nodded slowly.

'Enough said. I understand. I think you're wrong though. You're missing a big chance to show everyone who you really are and what you can do.'

'It's this way or not at all,' I said.

'Fine,' said Holly.

'Who will you be then, mate?' asked Artie.

I had this one. For years, I'd been drawing a cartoon of a pretty unique superhero. He couldn't fly, or shoot webs from his hands, and he certainly wasn't made of iron. He wasn't even a grown-up superhero. Some would find him boring. No, this pretty ordinary superhero was just a kid with one special power. He was great at radio. He was Radio Boy.

'I'm Radio Boy,' I said to Artie and Holly.

STEP 3:

IF YOUR SHOW IS SECRET THEN KEEP IT THAT WAY OR FACE THE REST OF YOUR LIFE BEHIND BARS (SLANG FOR PRISON)

We had to protect our identities. If you or I wanted to really do this on the street then we would put on some disguises and outfits, maybe a fake beard and glasses. On the radio, it's not so easy.

'You'll need to disguise your voice as well, Spike,' said Holly, casually. 'We'll need a vocal transmogrifier.'

'Yeah, of course.' (That was me.)

'Uh-huh.' (That was Artie, nodding.)

But Holly could clearly tell by our blank expressions that we had no idea what on earth she had just said.

'It's something you put on the microphone and it disguises your voice, alters it. You know, shifts it higher or lower. So no one would know it was you, Spike, or if Artie is talking, we could disguise his voice too.'

'How do we get a noodle transiter?' I asked.

'IT'S A V-O-C-A-L TRANS-MOGRIFIER! My dad will make us one. I'll just say it's for AV Club.'

This news did not reassure me. Holly's dad's newest invention was a phone for dogs. The dog would wear a small phone round its neck and while you were out you could call the dog and have a good old chat by yelling, 'WHO'S A GOOD BOY . . .?' to a terrified pooch. Like many inventions from Timothy Tate Enterprises, it had to be recalled after complaints of dogs needing canine counselling after just a few hours with the Dog Phone.

However, this time Holly's dad, Timothy Tate, struck gold.

Timbo Tate made us what will stand as his greatest invention yet: this thing was a beauty!

A couple of days later, Holly returned to my house, carrying a black box with a small, shiny knob.

'Here you go,' she said. 'This is a vocal transmogrifier.'

We needed to test this mysterious device. Which meant we needed to get into our studio. This would be the first time we'd attempted to sneak in through the secret back gate, to make it to our shed. This would be an important practice run to see how easy or hard it would be next week for real.

I waited until I knew Mum would be out at work.

'Quietly,' ordered Holly. Then she did some funny gestures from Army Cadets that apparently meant, 'open the gate with the key, Spike'. I worked that out after she had to whisper it, because I didn't understand her little hand movements.

I took the secret key Dad had given me from round my neck and unlocked the hidden gate. At first it wouldn't shift, after years of never being used. Then, finally, it flew open. We fought our way through the angry brambles in my garden jungle to the shed door. There was a shiny new padlock Dad had wisely fitted to keep out any unwelcome visitors – luckily, he'd given me a key for that too, last night.

We were in.

Holly quickly went to work switching everything on, and various red and green lights started blinking awake.

'You excited, mate?' whispered Artie. He'd bought some out-of-date cakes along for the occasion.

'Yes,' I said. 'But what if no one listens?'

Suddenly, this had gone from being a great idea and adventure to a reality that made me scared. Scared that I might not actually be that good at being a DJ, just like almost every other area in

my life. Scared no one would even bo
in and I'd look stupid to my friends, Dad
Taggart.

'Well, I think you're great, Spike,' said Artie. 'This is what you're meant to do. The school needs you as well. Why don't you just see it as . . . you know, a funny little thing we're going to try for a few weeks, no big deal. Just us shooting the breeze like we always do.'

He was right. I was building this up to be some HUGE life-changing event when I didn't need to.

Artie patted me softly on the shoulder. It meant just as much as his reassuring words. I felt like hugging him but DIDN'T as that would have been WEIRD.

'Ready to try Dad's creation, Spike?' Holly asked.

We all sat round the studio desk and put headphones on. This voice disguiser had to work, otherwise there'd be no show. I had to remain the

how spies must feel

over.

on my 'mic' (technical

phone) and felt a jolt of

nob and pick how you want your new secret voice to sound, Spike,' instructed Holly. I moved it a bit and spoke.

'Hi, this is Spike,' is what I said. But what came out was:

'NNNNNNNNNNNNMMMPPPPPP HHHGGGGGGGGGGGG.'

We all burst out laughing. It sounded really, really deep and slowed down, like one of the messages a kidnapper leaves in a scary movie.

'Well, I can't use that voice – no one would listen.'

'Move it again,' suggested Holly. I did, this time way more to the left.

Now I sounded REALLY, REALLY HIGH-

PITCHED! Like a chipmunk on helium.

More giggles.

'Shhhhhhhhh!' Holly pleaded.

I moved the shiny dial again.

'Hi . . . one two . . . one two . . . oh, this sounds great! How cool is this . . . NOW I'm a DJ!'

Everyone nodded in agreement. Holly, the new super-producer, came round with a pen and made a mark where the dial needed to be for 'me' in disguise.

I sounded a bit older, a bit deeper. Manly. If Katherine Hamilton heard this, well, it could be a game changer *and* a voice changer. I wanted to carry the black box of wonder (vocal thingy, more technical lingo) with me everywhere.

'Hey, wouldn't it be cool for me to say 'yes' during the class register tomorrow morning? Freak everyone out,' I said. We were all smiling, and in that moment I felt happier than I had in a very long time.

STEP 4:
ADVERTISE YOUR SHOW

This started badly. Learn from our mistakes: if you want to make flyers and leave them around the school, telling everyone about your new secret show, then get the details right.

Look at this, and spot the mistake:

Martin Harris came up to me in the corridor – never a pleasant experience.

'You know anything about this?' he snarled, thrusting one of our flyers in my face.

'N-n-no,' I stuttered. He was huge. His eyes were full of anger and evil, if eyes can do that.

'Nah, didn't think you would. None of you spods would have the guts.' He looked at Holly and Artie. Only Holly stared back at him. Unblinking. Probably working out how to neutralise him using just her school bag and a ruler.

'Well, anyone who tries to compete with me is going to be in big trouble. My dad will see to that.' He marched off, after throwing the flyer on the floor and stamping on it.

We looked at each other and started giggling. We weren't even on air yet and we were making an impact.

STEP 5:

SECURE ALL THE EQUIPMENT YOU NEED

You can do an internet radio show with just a laptop and microphone. But we (well, Artie) wanted to play music on our show, and not just music but old records, which meant even more equipment. Which meant another heist. On our 'shopping' list was a turntable for Artie to play the music on – but we also needed a phone so we could take calls on the show. Yep. Our show was going to have kids calling in. We were going to blow Merit Radio away.

My old hospital radio security pass was going to come in handy. I knew the station shut down during the afternoon so this would be when we could sneak in and 'borrow' the turntable from the spare studio they had. I would give it back once we'd saved enough pocket money to get one from a car boot sale. Three pounds should do it.

I was concerned that there might be CCTV cameras and we would be spotted. I was pretty sure they wouldn't miss the turntable as it was hardly used, but I didn't want to take any chances. Mum would be working at the hospital and that could ruin everything.

So I got my pocket money and went to a charity shop to get some clothes to wear as disguises. Then into the fancy-dress shop to get a few extra props. I texted the gang to meet at mine.

'Spike, why would an eleven-year-old girl have a beard?' Holly asked, holding out the fake beards I'd got for all of us.

'Well, this way, if anyone *does* see anything then they'll think they're looking for three old people: men with beards. It's perfect. Take these as well,' I offered as I handed them a walking stick each.

'Um . . .' said Artie.

157

'Perfect,' I said, taking a step back.

Holly had a fake beard, a big brown jumper and brown trousers all rolled up, plus the walking stick and fake glasses. Artie also looked like an old man . . . ish.

Unfortunately, his fake beard wasn't the same as ours, because the shop had run out of black ones. I'd had to get him a white Father Christmas one (it came with a complimentary jingle bell hat). I'd also found a grey cardigan and yellow trousers for him. What with his walking stick, he looked . . . well, I have to be honest and I never said anything to him of course, but he looked like he'd escaped from a special unit for crazy people.

'I look like a crazy tramp, Spike,' moaned Artie.

'No, you don't. We look like old people, and that's perfect.' I caught a glimpse of myself in the mirror as we left. Black beard, fake glasses and nose, pink cardigan and black shiny tracksuit pants that were way too big for me. Perfect.

We got on the bus and headed over to the hospital radio station. Just getting on the bus caused quite a stir. As we went to pay, the bus driver told us, 'It's free on Fridays for OAPs.'

It was working!

The bus driver was most fascinated by Holly. I guess it was a bit odd that an old man with a beard would have bright blond hair, but maybe this old guy dyed his beard as he was in a jazz band.

We shuffled along with what we thought was the slow, bent-over walk of old people. Artie started to really get into character by shouting and waving his walking stick at cars that were driving too fast on the road outside the hospital.

'Slow down, you young hooligans!' he said, in his best impression of an elderly man.

As we approached the hospital radio station, I got my security pass ready to swipe through the huge double doors. These were bigger than normal doors as often patients on beds came through them. The pass worked and the doors opened. My heart was beating really fast. Holly was sweating so much her beard started to slip.

We quickly snuck downstairs as I'd done on many Saturdays. It didn't take long to get into the spare studio, and I put Artie on watch in the deserted hallway. Holly and I unplugged the turntable gently and then the phone as well.

'Where's your bag?' Holly whispered to me.

Oh no. I'd forgotten it in all my preparations.

'SPIKE! YOU DON'T HAVE A BAG? WE CAN'T JUST CARRY THESE OUT OF HERE!' Holly yelled. Wide-eyed with panic.

Think, Spike, think. Stay calm.

An idea hit me. I gathered the team and told them what we needed to do. They resisted at first, but I said we didn't have any choice. It was either this or leave now with nothing. I told them to stay there, and I went and fetched what we needed.

Artie got into position and made himself comfortable as we headed for the lift. All three of us were shaking with a mixture of wild excitement at what we were trying to do, and terror at the idea of getting caught.

Artie was lying on a hospital bed under a blanket. Under that blanket were also the 'borrowed' items from the station. Genius, eh? Holly and I pushed the bed along, with Artie making convincing groaning noises. He looked like he was suffering from a very rare medical condition that caused his stomach to take on a peculiar shape – similar to a turntable and phone. We pressed the ground-floor button in the lift. My fingers were shaking. Doing the radio show was going to be calm and relaxing compared to all this. The lift doors opened, and now we were just metres away from the outside world and freedom.

Then I spotted a major problem. The gnome was heading towards us!

'Oh no,' I mumbled under my fake beard.

'What?' cried the others.

'It's the gnome, Graham Bingham. He works at the station!' I said through gritted teeth.

'ARRGHHHHHH,' Artie groaned, staying in character.

The human gnome, himself a beard-wearer, nodded in a concerned manner at the poor patient on the bed. He stopped to chat.

OH, double triple no.

I was going to have a heart attack and end up on the bed myself.

'Don't worry, sir, you're in the best place – which ward are you taking him to?' asked the gnome. This wasn't good. It was very, very bad.

I could only remember one ward name, the one my mum runs.

'Barnabus,' I fired back. Maybe we would be OK.

'The children's ward?' replied Graham the Gnome, quite correctly. It was at this exact moment that Holly's beard just quit on the spot and fell to the ground.

What happened next was like something out of a movie. A bad one. Me, Artie, Holly and the gnome just stared at one another, our brains trying to process what had happened. I took immediate action and yelled, 'GO!' as I ran off, pushing Artie on his bed as fast as I could.

It took a few more seconds for the gnome to process this latest development. He yelled, 'Stop there!' and headed after us.

He would've caught us for sure, but then

something amazing happened. Not looking where he was going, and chasing after us in hot pursuit, he ran into a hospital stretcher that was carrying a properly ill person and landed right on top of them and their two broken legs. Hearing the screams, I looked back to see a hospital doctor throwing the gnome on to the floor and shouting swear words at him. We rounded the corner at speed.

'Quick, off the bed, Artie, there's a shop over there. Let's get a bag,' I ordered.

The heist was done. We were exhausted.

A few days later, our local paper featured this small story:

HOSPITAL BED PILE-UP

Police were called on Friday afternoon to a local hospital after a patient with two broken legs was attacked by Graham Bingham, a hospital radio DJ. Mr Bingham, 57, was cautioned for wasting police time and for 'running in a medical area'. Mr Bingham told the police he was chasing three people who he thought were trying to escape from the psychiatric ward. A search of the immediate area found a walking stick and a fake beard. Mr Bingham has been temporarily suspended from the station.

CHAPTER 16

How to do the world's worst radio show

My heart jumped on Monday morning before school when Mum said, 'Something is going on . . .'

The next few seconds were a blur. How had she found out? We'd got so far, and now it was all over?

'. . . at Number 72, the Fishers',' she continued, and walked over to her observation post at the front-room curtains, her favourite.

I breathed a quiet sigh of relief. However, it really was going to be a miracle if Mum never found out about what was happening in the shed.

Merit Radio launched that day during the lunch break. I say *launched*, but it would be fairer to say it just arrived, without any warning or introduction. It was about as welcome as a cross-country run on a freezing-cold December day. We were 'encouraged' (forced) to listen in the school dining hall as it was blasted out from speakers above our tables. We had to be forced, as no one in their sane mind would've listened to that rubbish by choice. People were laughing into their lukewarm school dinners at what they heard and, believe me, 'Merit Radio' wasn't trying to be funny. It was deadly, boringly serious. Like those TV documentaries your dad falls asleep in front of, about how glass or contact lenses are made. In fact, either of those would be infinitely more interesting than Merit Radio.

If they'd just played ten minutes of someone scraping their fingernails down a blackboard, it would have been less awful. You'll be thinking, 'Oh, Spike is exaggerating because he's angry he wasn't picked to do the show.'

WELL, STOP THINKING THAT RIGHT NOW.

So, to record everything for future radio historians who one day might want to google the words, 'What is the world's worst radio show?', I have noted what went down. I've made this into a report and listed everything that happened. With comments.

MONDAY

1pm

LOCATION: DINING HALL

ST BRENDA'S SCHOOL LUNCH BREAK

LUNCH: SHEPHERD'S PIE (*or jacket potato and beans for the vegetarian kids*)

1.01pm

The national anthem starts playing over the PA system so loudly and suddenly it makes us all jump out of our skins. A few of us actually look round to see if the Queen of England has joined us all for lunch (she would've loved the shepherd's pie). People look at each other, confused. Is the world ending?

1.04pm

National anthem ends.

A high-pitched whistling sound is now heard, so piercing it makes you wince. It means a microphone isn't being used properly. AMATEURS!

Muffled, angry yelling can be heard in the background; the voice is unmistakably that of Mr Harris, aka Fish Face, the headmaster. Clearly, he is the producer. Lucky them. No doubt his angry red face is currently screaming at some kid to sort the problem out. This is wonderful. The puppet master controlling his puppets. And muppets.

'Good afternoon, you are listening to the first ever show on Merit Radio . . .'

A small, forced round of applause breaks out in the studio. (No doubt 'encouraged' at gunpoint by Fish Face). It's starting to sound as if the presenters are being held hostage.

'I'm Martin Harris,' says Martin Harris, finally, 'and it gives me enormous pleasure to launch the first ever radio station for St Brenda's. We will be here every lunchtime to celebrate all that's great about St Brenda's school. No better way to start this show than with some live music. Stephen Greaves passed his grade one trumpet yesterday and will now play for us . . .'

1.06pm

The sound of a child being forcibly pushed towards a microphone. Then a case being clicked open. Wow. Radio gold, Fish Face.

1.07pm

Someone can be heard hissing, 'HURRY UP!'

Producer Fish Face, obviously being a very chilled and supportive producer.

1.08pm

I'm no trumpet expert, and I've no doubt a trumpet was being played, but to me it sounded like someone trying to inflate the world's largest balloon. No notes, just the huffing and puffing of a small, terrified child, trying desperately to blow into a trumpet to make it work. Only the occasional *parp* could be heard.

1.09pm and fifty-three seconds

No more of trumpet boy. I fear Fish Face has thrown him out of the nearest window.

1.10pm

Martin Harris is talking again, probably with his dad's hand up his backside controlling him.

'You are listening to the GREAT MERIT RADIO...'

More forced applause in the studio: Martin's ape mates must be there, knuckles scraping the ground.

'Now every day we will read out the names of pupils who have achieved high grades, merits or good exam results. Here are today's successful pupils, and to play some more live music is St Brenda's head of music, Miss Wicker, while I do this...'

Forced applause. Obviously, no more kids are to be trusted to play on air today after the failure of trumpet boy, currently being scraped off the pavement outside. Bring on old Mizzzzzzzzzzzzzzz Wicker. I'm not saying she's a crusty old woman, but she is.

1.12pm

Soft piano music is heard, the kind played in a dentist's waiting room.

PLINKLY PLONK, PLINKLY PLONK . . .

'Congratulations today on Merit Radio to . . .

'Mark Ellis, who got his gymnastics BAGA 3 award and apparently his work on the high bar was a delight!

'Lois Morris, who got a merit in her French project yesterday. Lois apparently wrote a poem about her pony, all in French. The poem was called . . . well, she is here right now to finish the show in some style . . .'

1.14pm

Piano playing ends suddenly. I fear Mizzzzzzz zzzzzzz Wicker may have had her hands slammed in the piano lid by Fish Face.

Shuffling. Silence. Very heavy breathing: must be poor Lois Morris, who has a sinus problem, and sadly can't breathe through her nose very well.

To really understand how this sounded, you'll need to pinch your nose and read this bit.

'My name is Lois Morris and this is my poem what I wrote in French about my pony; he is brown . . .

'*Mon Pony.*

'*Mon pony est appellé Monsieur Kit Kat.*'

Translation: my pony is called Mister Kit Kat.

'*Il est brun.*'

Translation: he is brown.

Now the last line I think Lois *wanted* to say was that she loves him, but what she actually says is:

'*Je serais ravie de le manger.*'

Which means: I'd like to eat him.

Give that kid a merit! A poem about eating your beloved brown pony – great show, guys!

Once word gets around the dining hall about what poor nasally-challenged Lois has actually said, laughter bounces around the room. I think I see a dinner lady smile.

No smiles over at the Merit Radio studio, I imagine.

Martin the Muppet is back, talking. Fish Face's big angry head must have exploded by now.

'We would like to apologise to any animal lovers listening. St Brenda's does not encourage the eating of your pets . . .'

A very long silence, then . . .

'. . . Well, that's it from us today. Back tomorrow with more on Merit Radio, when we will have a very interesting show-and-tell feature with Year Eight's Paul Allen, who is bringing in his collection of pebbles from over three beaches. Paul paints funny faces on his pebbles. Ha ha, oh, how funny. Hilarious, I'm sure. Well, we can hardly wait . . .'

Show ends.

Roll on Wednesday and my show.

CHAPTER 17

Elvis is in the shed

You know that funny feeling you get in your stomach when you're really excited about something? Well, times that by about a BILLION. People say, 'Oh, I've got butterflies in my stomach.' Well, this was more like a herd of excitable elephants rampaging wildly in there.

That's how I felt all that day at school.

It was Wednesday. Which meant Show One for the *SECRET SHED SHOW*.

That lunchtime, meanwhile, it was the *third* show for Merit Radio. You won't be surprised to know it was still awful. Just some highlights from today's award-dodging show:

1. Live music from Anne Anderson on her violin. It was either a violin we heard or a screaming cat having its claws cut.

2. Show-and-tell featuring Paul Allen and his stamp collection. Great radio that, talking about stamps you CAN'T ACTUALLY SEE.

3. Three cheers for Martin Mutant Harris who was presented with a trophy on his own show as captain of the school football team for winning some pointless game against our rival school. The chimp actually presented HIMSELF with the trophy while his gormless ape mates managed to drag their knuckles from the ground and give him a round of applause.

As I left school, Mr Taggart whispered, 'Good luck,' when he walked past me in the corridor. I guessed we could count on at least one listener. The flyers had been illegally posted around the school and the three of us had been stirring it up by asking everyone we knew, 'Hey, you heard about this new underground radio show that's really for us? Think I'll give it a go . . .'

Artie, Holly and I met at the top gate of our school after the home-time bell rang. We should've been at the AV Club – in fact, that's where Mum thought I was – but instead we were on our way to the secret gate at the bottom of my garden, and our destiny.

There wasn't much talking as we made our way to mine. Artie was probably struggling to talk, as he was huffing and puffing, carrying a big black case. Inside it were all the records for the day's show. You would've thought there was a million pounds in the case for the fuss Artie made over it all day. His backpack was also bulging under the strain of the extra cakes and buns he'd managed to smuggle out of Gateaux Chateau for us.

We finally reached the secret garden gate. The gateway to our adventure that *really was* about to begin. We had by now worked out the best route to take us through the bramble jungle while limiting blood loss and blindness. Every time we made it to the shed door safely, it felt like we were deep in the Amazon rainforest and had just discovered some ancient hidden temple, with a rusting lawnmower outside.

Once we were inside the shed, Holly did her business of getting everything turned on. Lights blinked awake and things started to hum. I took a few deep breaths to try to calm myself. I just tried to pretend that everything that was happening was normal and no big deal.

Holly remained standing as Artie and I sat down at the mixing desk. I was in front of all the faders and equipment, which I knew how to work with my eyes closed after all my time on hospital radio. Setting it up, though, fixing it: no idea. That was Holly's thing.

Artie was on my right-hand side by his mic.

'OK, team,' Holly said. 'Let's talk about our show today. It's going to be great.' She said this with such certainty I started to believe it.

I took out my notes with all my ideas for the first show.

'Well, I want a big song to open the show, Artie: a song that says right away who we are and what we're going to do.'

Artie nodded, smiling, and patted the stack of vinyl records knowingly.

'Then I will introduce myself and Artie. I won't call you Artie, obviously. I will refer to you as Ron.'

'What?' spluttered Artie, launching himself out of his chair, almost trampling on the bag crammed with cakes. He would've blown the shed apart with the cake explosion if that had happened.

'I'm Radio Boy, so you will need a secret name too, Artie,' I explained.

'I get that, but I'm not . . . RON! Ron is an old man's name. Radio Boy and *RON*? They'll just think some old git is in here with you. No, I will take inspiration from one of music's greats. I will be this guy . . .' He put on a deep, rolling American accent. '*Ladies and gentlemen, this is Elvis Presley*. People called him the "King of Rock and Roll" and from now on I will be known as Elvis in this studio.'

'Elvis . . .' I said, experimentally. 'I love it, Artie.'

'ELVIS!'

'Elvis, sorry. OK, well, that's sorted.' I looked at both of them. 'Listen . . . before we start the show, I want to say something. I want this show to really mean something for kids like us. I want it to be theirs. I want us to talk about things that really matter to us. You don't get that on ANY other radio show. Those shows are just for our parents, not us. Merit Radio isn't for us either. It belongs to Mr Harris. I'm not saying I'm not happy about Anne Anderson getting her grade one violin, but how is any of that going to help us when we have important questions that need answering? Like, why do our parents tell us lies?'

'Lies?' said Holly.

'Yeah,' I said. 'Did I ever tell you about my first bike? Do you know what my mum and dad told me? They swore blind it was a brand spanking new bike. I knew something wasn't quite right, though – maybe the odd flaking red paint revealing the name "Cupcake" along the frame. *Odd name for a boy's bike*, I thought.

'"Oh no, son, straight out of the bike factory,"

Dad reassured me. All lies! I found out it was my sister's old pink bike that my mum had got Dad to paint red.'

Artie laughed. 'My dad told me that when the ice-cream van came round and played its tune, that meant it had run out of ice creams,' he said. There was genuine sadness in his voice. As if a bottomless cake pit wasn't enough for him. I seriously think Artie's blood group must be icing.

'My mum told me that Santa is chubby because he eats naughty kids,' said Holly.

'This is all great,' I said. 'So, we'll get kids to call in with lies their parents have told them. Then, later on in the show, I will be . . . Fish Face.'

Holly and Artie frowned.

'Go on . . .' ventured Artie.

'Well, I will "interview" Mr Harris. But of course I will be both myself *and* Fish Face. Radio Boy will be chatting to Mr Harris, our lovely headmaster. Holly, can you flick the vocal trans . . .

transfer . . . the voice changer to go quickly from my setting to then making me, as Fish Face, sound like a sea monster? All *sloooooooow* and *blooooooobby*, like the man himself?'

'EASILY!' Holly fired back right away.

What a great team I had.

'OK, sorted then,' I said.

'Isn't that . . . going to make him really angry though?' said Artie.

'Oh, come on,' I said. 'Just the show existing is going to make him angry.'

'Hmm. I guess.'

'No one will know it's us though, will they, Spike?' said Holly. 'Secret. Like we agreed?'

'Absolutely,' I reassured them.

'OK,' said Holly. 'Artie, what about the music? What's our opener?'

'This, my friends, is going to be our first song to the world,' said Artie. 'We want a song that's really going to say what we are about on the *Secret Shed Show*, and this is it.'

Artie thrust a shiny black disc into our faces for us to read the central song label.

'"Revolution", by the legendary Beatles. Because this song says it all. We are going to start a revolution with this show, Spike.'

'Cool,' I said.

'All the songs have been carefully chosen for today's first ever show,' continued Artie. 'After the show, Holly, I thought we could even post the track listing on our website . . .' As Artie spoke, he took an enormous bite of his doughnut. Some jam spilled on to the Beatles album cover.

'. . . and I'll start a *Secret Shed Show* Spotify playlist!' said Holly.

'Three minutes from show time,' she added.

I took my headphones from my bag. Taped to them was a little note. It was from Dad.

Just do what you do, son. Have fun. Dad xxx

Despite the bike lies, he's a good dad. Sometimes.

I tested my mic and nervously checked a few times that my deep voice disguiser setting was on. We tested Artie's too. Holly tried a few different settings before Artie was satisfied.

'Elvis is in the building,' he said.

'It's a shed,' said Holly.

Artie rolled his eyes. 'Philistine.'

I was ready.

Elvis was ready.

Holly took out her bedside alarm clock and placed it in front of me. 'When it's four o'clock, you start the show and launch our pirate ship. Good luck, Radio Boy.'

CHAPTER 18

The Secret Shed Show launches and sets the world on fire

I stared at my mic. My mouth was as dry as Dad's Sunday roast, where he somehow manages to make the beef taste like old shoes. As if sensing this, Holly handed me a glass of water. Artie just sat there, looking as chilled as ever. That helped too. I didn't need both of us shaking with nerves.

I sat in silence, watching the second hand on the clock, every tick seeming to cause my heart to beat louder and faster. I took a deep breath as the clock hands moved to four o'clock exactly.

It was time.

I pushed my fader button up, and a sign flashed red in the studio.

'Hi, I'm Radio Boy and this is the *Secret Shed Show*. Streaming live across the world on www dot secret shed show dot com.

'We aren't about who got the highest grades and the most merits, or trumpet recitals.

'We all try but sometimes we fail.

'Who said we have to be the best at everything?

'Maybe you aren't top of the class or captain of the A team.

'Maybe you don't think you fit in.

'Well, you fit in here.

'We don't have a fish-faced headmaster controlling us.

'We are going to talk about our older brothers and sisters and mutant apes at school that make our lives a nightmare.

'I don't even know if this show is really going to work or if we can do it, but maybe, I dunno, together we can try and figure it out.

'Oh, and we rock.'

I pressed PLAY. The loud squealing guitars of 'Revolution' by the Beatles rang out loud.

I closed my fader, turning off the mics. The big red MIC LIVE went out just above the flowerpots.

Elvis patted me on the back, as did Holly. I wasn't nervous any more. This all just felt, I dunno, right. Like it was meant to be.

The record came to an end. Time for us to speak again.

'THE BEATLES'
"REVOLUTION" ON THE
SECRET SHED SHOW.
I'M RADIO BOY AND WITH
ME IS ELVIS...'
"UH-HUH."
'WE GO TO ST BRENDA'S
SCHOOL AND WANTED TO DO
OUR OWN RADIO SHOW THAT
DIDN'T BORE YOU TO TEARS
LIKE MERIT RADIO.

WE CAN'T DO IT WITHOUT YOU THOUGH – WE WANT YOU TO BE PART OF THE SHOW. YOU CAN CONTACT US ON OUR WEBSITE. SAY HELLO AND LEAVE YOUR COMMENTS. OR YOU CAN EMAIL US, OR CALL US ON 07900 555 2368 TODAY. WE WANT TO HEAR ABOUT THE LIES YOUR PARENTS HAVE TOLD YOU.

I then told my story of parental fraud with the hand-me-down girl's bike. Artie told his ice-cream van story, and then it was time for another song. David Bowie with 'Rebel Rebel'. Perfect. Never heard it before in my life, but it was brilliant.

Holly pointed at the screen of the laptop.

Something amazing was happening. Our website was slowly coming to life with comments. First just one, two, three. People were listening! Then four or five comments . . . It was small, still, but they were there and it was a start.

Then the phone rang in the shed. We all jumped out of our skins. The shed studio team froze.

Finally, Holly picked it up. 'Hello, the *Secret Shed Show*?'

She listened intently, smiled, then said, 'Can you please wait there? You'll be live on air after this song.' This is what real producers say to callers! I was in heaven. In a shed, a shed heaven.

'Tom is on line one, Radio Boy,' said Holly, 'and

has a funny story about a lie his dad told him.'

The song faded.

'This is the *Secret Shed Show*,' I said. 'That was David Bowie and "Rebel Rebel". That's proper music, Merit Radio. Later on today we have some recipes for the best way to cook and eat your pets, inspired by Monday's show on Merit Radio.'

'Mine is a *ham-ster and cheese toastie*,' chipped in Elvis.

'Well, Elvis, I love *cat-atouille*,' I replied.

'Of course, the *Secret Shed Show* does not support the cooking and eating of beloved family pets, unless it's a cat as they are quite irritating . . . I'm joking! Anyway, on the line we have Tom. Hi, Tom.'

'Hi, Radio Boy, loving the show!'

I didn't know what to say. 'Um . . . yes . . . thank you, Tom . . . Tom, you are the first ever caller on the *Secret Shed Show* and you've won a . . . prize!'

What did I say that for? I quickly scanned the shed to see what I could give away. I wasn't really sitting on a goldmine of luxury prizes in there. My eyes darted around furiously from flowerpots, to weedkiller sprays, to rusty old nails. Inspiration hit me.

'Tom, you have won an old paintbrush!'

'A . . . *paintbrush*?' Tom sounded underwhelmed.

'It's a highly coveted golden paintbrush we will only give away to our first ever caller. Elvis, can you start painting it gold for Tom?'

'What? Yeah, I guess so,' Elvis said with a face that if it was an emoji would look like this:

He obviously didn't get my genius.

'So, Tom, what's the lie your parents told you?'

'My mum told me that the smoke detectors around our house were in fact cameras that went directly to the North Pole and Father Christmas so he could see if you were misbehaving.'

Holly and I laughed. Artie looked confused.

'What's up, Elvis?' I asked.

'My dad told me that too. I thought it was true. And that you only get a thousand words to speak every month: once you get to that limit, you gotta wait until the next month to speak again.'

I started the next song. Somebody called the Beastie Boys came blasting out of the shed speakers, urging us to fight for our right to party. The little shed was rocking.

Right then, I knew I'd remember this moment for the rest of my life. I was happy. It was working. I could do it. Some people were listening.

Now it was time to really stir things up.

'That was the Beastie Boys and "(You Gotta) Fight for Your Right (to Party)". We now have a very special guest. Yes, it's the headmaster of St Brenda's school, Mr Harris . . .'

Holly's hands were now a blur of action as she flicked between my 'Radio Boy' setting (which she'd written on the box) and a new one labelled 'Sea Monster' for Mr Harris.

'Hi, Radio Boy, and thanks for having me on the *Secret Shed Show*,' said Mr Harris in his best sea monster voice.

'Hi, Mr Harris. Tell me, what's new with you?'

'Well, Radio Boy, I have a show of my own called Merit Radio. Have you heard it? It sounds like this . . .'

I fired off the sound effect I had lined up. The sound of a very loud, rip-roaring fart. Elvis fell off his chair laughing.

'You know my son Martin?' continued Fish Face. 'He presents the show. Well, he's really a chimpanzee dressed as a boy. Today I caught him trying to organise his M&Ms into alphabetical order.'

Holly spat her drink out.

'He's a chimpanzee but he presents a radio show?' I said.

'Oh, I taught him to talk,' said Mr Harris. 'He's just not potty-trained yet. So the studio can get a little bit . . . messy.'

'TMI, Mr Harris! TMI!'

'You know why I look the way I do?' asked Mr Harris.

'No.'

'Because I was made in the science lab at school many years ago and the experiment went very wrong. I'm part man, part fish.'

'That's very sad, sir,' I offered in sympathy.

'Well, on the plus side, I have gills so I can breathe underwater in the bath; on the downside, I have a goldfish memory . . . who are you again?'

The studio erupted into laughter. I hoped our few listeners were doing the same.

Now time for Fish Face to say goodbye.

'Well, that's it from me for today, Radio Boy.

I have to go and have my tea, which is a huge plate of manure to keep my breath smelling this bad.'

I played our last song. Elvis had picked something by someone called Pink Floyd. I could hear the lyrics, another great choice from my head of music.

'Hey, teacher, leave those kids alone.'

More comments were coming in on the website from people who'd heard the last bit.

Bieberfan2003 **Amazing! Lol.**

Lottysmith **Can't believe what I'm hearing! You are in BIG TROUBLE when they find out who you are! Keep up the great show.**

Alexroberts **Too funny! He does look like a fish! Omg lol.**

'That's it from us on the *Secret Shed Show*,' I said. 'We will be back same time next week. Please spread the word, leave us messages and email us about anything you want. I hope you enjoyed listening. I'm Radio Boy and this has been the *Secret Shed Show*.'

The first show was over. We had started something. Quite *what* we had started, none of us really knew. We all looked at each other. Our faces were glowing.

There was no better way to enjoy the moment than with a delicious doughnut each. Only three days past their sell-by date.

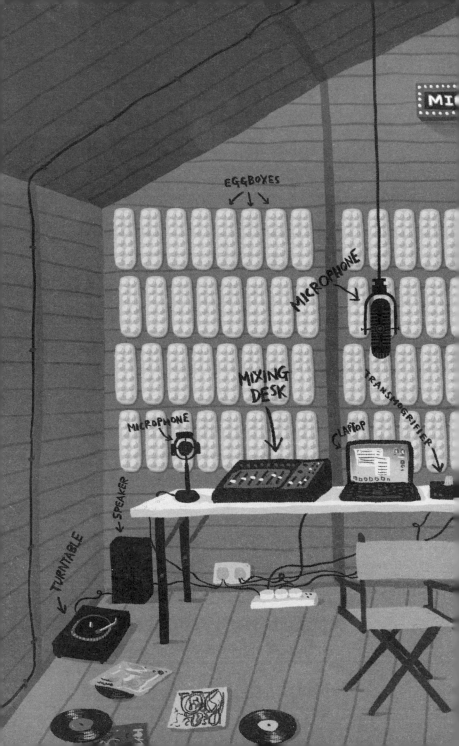

CHAPTER 19

The rise of Radio Boy

After that first show, everything was a bit of a blur.

The weeks flew by, and every week we would get more and more comments on our website. Ten became fifty became ninety. We were getting hundreds after we did our third show. News gets around any school quickly, like the latest funny viral video involving cats falling in toilets. I guess the *Secret Shed Show* was now going viral, which sounds like an illness but isn't.

The first thing that told me the *Secret Shed Show* was a *real* hit was when I saw this graffiti in the boys' toilets at school:

It felt amazing! *Wait until I tell the others we're officially graffiti famous*, I thought.

Then my heart sank a bit when I saw what was underneath it:

I'M RADIO BOY.

I felt like scribbling on there:

No, I, Spike Hughes, am Radio Boy

It was hard staying anonymous and in the shadows. I was so, so happy the show was getting bigger and bigger every week, but it was awful not getting all the glory. Is that wrong? It was like being an awesome striker in a football team, but playing with a bag over your head. Not sure if that's a good example, but it's the only one I can think of right now.

OK: imagine being a superhero and not being able to tell everyone it was you. I knew what it must be like to be Iron Man, aka Tony Stark, or Bruce Wayne, aka Batman. If the three of us ever met up, we would have *so* much to talk about.

Looking back over the shows in the last few weeks, there had been some awesome bits.

We had done a feature called Fish Face Idol. We asked people to call in and do their best impressions of our headmaster, Mr Harris. The winner got a framed photo: a face swap of Mr Harris and a blobfish, which looked like this:

A few shows later, inspired by a particularly depressing Merit Radio show where the usual A-graders got loud and noisy congratulations after our big exams, I decided to have my own version of school merits. Ours were for your 'Best Failures'. People tweeted in using #bestfailures. Others called; some emailed. This was the biggest thing we'd done. Some of my favourites:

- Johnny called in, saying he'd spent two days glueing together an amazing model of the Millennium Falcon. Once he finished it, he enjoyed a victory lap of honour round his bedroom and then, due to his tiredness after his marathon efforts, he accidentally sat on it.

- Caitlin called in, saying that when she was hungry the other day she ate some brightly coloured biscuits that were in the kitchen. Ten minutes later, her mum came in and asked where the dog biscuits were that she'd just left on the kitchen table . . .

- Danielle called in. She texted her grandad 'Happy Birthday You', but due to autocorrect he got 'Happy Birthday Poo'.

But the best was this email:

To: studio@secretshedshow.com
From: jamie king
Subject: Best Failure

Hey, Radio Boy,

Please can you, Elvis and the mysterious lady in the background keep doing this show? I look forward to Wednesdays now — your show means I've made it halfway through the week. I hate school and this keeps me sane.

My best failure was when I tried to make a home-made zipwire ride in my kitchen while my parents were having a lie-in one Sunday morning. I used some washing line from the garden. I attached one end to the kitchen light on the ceiling and the other to the fridge door. I stood on a kitchen stool and wrapped a tea towel over the washing line and grabbed with both hands and launched myself off.

My parents, after being rudely woken by a terrible crashing noise, rushed downstairs to find me on the kitchen floor along with most of the ceiling!

Artie got me to play a song called 'Crash' by the Primitives for Jamie.

After that, we had another good comment, but not surprisingly he didn't want to tell us his name:

Hi, Radio Boy!

I made a Valentine's card, put it through the letter box of the girl I liked. Two days later I found out I'd been tricked and that it wasn't her address. It was one of the school dinner ladies, Big Brenda.

To this day she always winks at me and gives me extra mash.

So many people were talking about the show; in fact, WE GOT PUT IN THE LOCAL PAPER!

OK, it wasn't the front page (actually page 27, right by the adverts for converting your loft into a room cheaply), but we were FAMOUS!

Dad crept upstairs with the newspaper tucked dramatically up his woolly jumper. You'd have thought it contained top-level government secrets. He waved page 27 in front of my face with a huge grin.

WHO IS THE UNKNOWN BOY DJ?

There is a mystery beaming into the bedrooms of children all over town. A secret radio show, live from a shed somewhere in one of our neighbourhoods, has become a big hit. All that's known is that the stars of the show, 'Radio Boy' and his sidekick 'Elvis', are probably pupils at St Brenda's school. They are joined in their budget wooden shack of a studio by a girl, the producer of the show, also thought to be a pupil.

Every Wednesday night they broadcast to the world from their website www.secretshedshow.com. Speculation about their identities is feverish, yet they remain anonymous by using voice-disguising equipment.

Howard Wright, breakfast show host on Kool FM, said, 'Go, Radio Boy! If I was a kid now, I would have wanted to do this! I'm gonna tune in to see if I have some competition!'

The headmaster at St Brenda's refused to comment when we contacted him. We did, however, hear some bizarre sobbing and murmuring noises when we called. Rumours are the show has not gone down well with the headmaster, as his son runs the school's official station, Merit Radio. Sounds like Mr Harris has a radio war on his hands. You can hear the *Secret Shed Show* at www.secretshedshow.com.

'You've done it!' said Dad as he proudly patted my shoulder and crept back out of my bedroom (quietly, in case Mum heard).

I was dizzy with excitement reading the article. I had to sit down I was so stunned and happy. I was famous! Only a few weeks ago I had been fired by Barry 'Bazza' Dingle and replaced by a human garden gnome. Now I was winning for once.

Not only that but HOWARD WRIGHT (the bestest DJ ever) had heard about me.

I read the whole thing again, especially the line where he said, 'I'm gonna tune in.'

MY MIND WAS OFFICIALLY BLOWN. It could only get better from here. Couldn't it?

CHAPTER 20

HOMEWORK HELL

'So, *Secret Shed Show* listeners, there almost wasn't a show tonight due to the crazy amount of homework we all have.'

I wasn't lying: Mr Harris was in a bad mood – I had a feeling it might have had something to do with the *Secret Shed Show* – and he was taking it out on the whole school by making sure we had extra homework. Hours and hours every night, all week and over the weekend. There was no escape.

'Can someone please explain the benefit of writing a rap about the Vikings?' chipped in Artie aka Elvis. 'Since when has rap been a way of learning?'

Seriously, this was last week's history homework. Our teacher, Mr Swift, trying to be down with da kidz. Next he'd be coming into school with a baseball cap on backwards and covered in bling.

'Yeah, why rap music? Why not opera?' I said.

'*Oh, woe is me, my axe has gone blunt . . .*' warbled Artie in his best opera-singer impression.

'Ha!' I said. 'Want to hear some of my Viking lyrics I didn't hand in?'

'Sure!' Artie and Holly nodded.

'Right, I'll read them out after this.' I played a song. The show was really going well tonight. Artie and Holly were enjoying themselves and I couldn't have been happier. The last time I had been this happy was in Artie's tree house during the summer holidays, when the three of us spent the night in it. Artie's dad hadn't given his only child any normal tree house. This was more a palace placed in a tree. A tree palace. This luxurious hideaway had:

1. A TV
2. A fridge
3. A telescope that NASA would envy
4. Armchairs with a remote control to adjust their settings
5. Some ancient unit that played those old-fashioned records Artie collected
6. Air hockey
7. A popcorn machine
8. A telephone
9. A butler

OK. I made the last one up. But it was amazing. The only thing missing was an elevator to take you up to it.

The song ended. I put our mics on and the big red MIC LIVE sign lit up.

'Hi, it's the unknown DJ Radio Boy here on the *Secret Shed Show*. With me, as ever, is Elvis, my music man, and of course the Secret Producer. Say hello, team.'

'HI!' they both said.

'So these are some of my Viking rap lyrics I had to reject . . . Elvis, could you beatbox to provide some suitable backing music . . .?'

Artie did indeed start laying down a drumbeat with just the power of his mouth. It sounded more like he was having severe breathing difficulties, but it was all I needed.

'Here we go . . . My Viking rap . . . HIT IT . . .

'I got a axe, I got a mace
One swing and I'll destroy yo face
Let's go, Viking
It's better than biking

Get on a horse
And join the Norse.'

My Viking rap got a shed studio round of applause, and I played another song. I could see we had some calls coming in. Artie and I looked at each other and grinned; we didn't even need to say anything – we *knew* that was funny.

Holly held up the phone. 'I've got a girl on the line who has a homework problem she wants some help with,' she said.

'Great, stick her on air then,' I replied. The show was alive tonight. Comments flooding in on the site, about hating homework, about the Viking rap, about whether Elvis could maybe sing some more opera. I could feel the adrenaline rush it was giving me. After spending so much time mumbling to myself and hugging the walls at school, I was now in the spotlight. People were finally listening to me.

The song was coming to an end. Time to chat to our caller.

'Hey, Radio Boy here. It's your *Secret Shed Show*! Time to chat to someone who's called in. Hello?'

'Hi, Radio Boy, Katherine here.'

OMG. Be still my beating heart. This, I could tell from just five words, was KATHERINE HAMILTON. The girl I wanted to marry. I froze. Artie kicked me under the table.

'Ow!' It got my attention back to the live radio show. *Be cool, Spike, be cool. You are Radio Boy.*

'Yes . . . um . . . great . . . What a lovely name you have, Katherine.' *WHAT A LOVELY NAME YOU HAVE, KATHERINE? THAT'S THE BEST I CAN DO?*

I wanted to hit myself in the face. With a Viking mace.

'Thanks,' purred Katherine Hamilton. This could be the start of something. Holly threw her arms up in the air, clearly not impressed with my on-air flirting with a caller.

'How can the *Secret Shed Show* help?' I asked. *That's better, Spike. Professional.*

'Well, firstly, can I say how much I love this show?'

I almost fainted. She loved me. The show, I mean. But . . .

'Th-th-th-th-thanks,' I stuttered.

'I hope you can help. This other history homework we have, about the Queen and our royal family. Anyone else struggling with it?'

Artie and Holly groaned at the mere thought of this homework, handed to us just a few hours earlier. An assignment about why we have a Queen and something-something about a 'monarchy'. All I know is Mr Harris has a big picture of her in his office so she must be important. To boring people.

'Yeah, sounds like a job for Wikipedia,' I said.

'It's so boring though! I mean, really boring.

What can we do?' Katherine Hamilton asked ME.

I needed to come up with something here. I needed to impress her. I, Radio Boy, could not let my future wife down.

'Got it!' I yelled.

'What?' replied an excited Katherine.

'Let's make it WAY more interesting with a game.'

'Oh, goody! I love games.' Again, be still, my beating heart.

'Great. Well, I'm going to give everyone a phrase that they have to try and work into their assignment. Whoever does it the best wins a prize.'

I had stolen this idea from my favourite DJ, Howard 'Howie' Wright – and the time when he got his listeners to try to slip the word 'cowpat' into letters printed in the newspaper.

'Great idea! What's the phrase?' said Artie.

'*Fish Face*. Aka Mr Harris.'

'That's so naughty!' said Katherine Hamilton. 'I love it. I'm going to go and do it right now. Don't forget it's due in tomorrow. Thanks, Radio Boy, you're the best.'

I was 'the best' – it was official. Like a seal of approval. My head felt dizzy. I wanted a T-shirt made with 'the best' on it.

'Well, that was truly sickening, Spike,' said Holly, when the mics were off, bringing me back down to earth abruptly.

'Yeah, sorry. It's just Katherine Hamilton and I really have something, I think. A connection. You heard it. Didn't you?'

'She was using you, Radio Boy. Like she does everyone.'

Artie spoke up. 'You made it weird, but great save with the Fish Face challenge. I wonder if anyone will actually do it. I will obviously.'

It turned out Artie wasn't the only one though: quite a few took up my challenge.

So much so, in fact, that Mr Harris got wind of it and called an emergency assembly at school two days later.

CHAPTER 21

Fish and Face

Artie, Holly and I all exchanged nervous looks as we made our way to assembly.

Once we had all been quietened down, Mr Harris marched on to the stage. It was the little things that gave away the fact he wasn't the happiest. The red angry face that looked like a dog chewing a wasp. The fact that he appeared to be muttering to himself. Then I saw what he was carrying.

He reached the middle of the hall and turned to face us. No time for niceties like 'Hello, children' or 'Good morning'.

'This is OUR QUEEN,' he spat, and held up the framed picture from his office of Her Royal Highness the Queen of England. 'And she deserves our respect! This incredible woman raises millions of pounds for charity and works hard every day for this great country. She is not an object for pathetic PRANKS.'

Some spit came flying out when he yelled 'PRANKS' and landed on the face of poor Joshua Wilson. He would now be forever tainted by this spittle. No longer just Joshua Wilson: from that moment he became Spit Face. RIP Joshua Wilson.

More yelling from Mr Harris.

'How is this funny?' he screeched as he held up a load of our assignments and began reading from them.

Oh no.

'Elizabeth II has been Queen of England since 1952. In a certain light, some say she has a fish face.

'The Queen owns four corgi dogs. Her two favourites are Fish and Face.'

We had all been trying to suppress our laughter, but couldn't any longer. A few kids snort-laughed. Mr Harris was not giggling. He was staring madly at us, his eyes bulging, like a fish you might say.

'I know who's behind this. A very sad individual in a garden shed. Someone calling himself Radio Boy. He has polluted your fresh, innocent minds and committed an act of treason against Her Majesty the Queen.' Mr Harris looked apologetically at his framed portrait of the monarch.

'A silly game that you will all pay the price for now. You will receive DOUBLE homework for the next week.' There wasn't any sniggering now. The assembly went very, very quiet as every single kid there grimaced at the thought of EVEN more homework. Double!

'I know Radio Boy is one of you. He may be in this room right now.' Mr Harris was walking around now, looking at each and every one of us. No one could bear to hold eye contact with him, for fear of him stealing their soul. My insides turned icy cold; the room felt as if it was closing in on me. Could he smell me? Through his fish-face gills?

'Hear me now, Radio . . . BOY. Hand yourself in and I will show due leniency and only suspend you for a week.'

Suspend me? That was nothing compared to what Mum would do to me if I *got* suspended. I could just hear her now. '*My Spike, SUSPENDED! What will people say? Do you have to wear an ankle tag like criminals under house arrest do?*'

'I'll say one last thing,' went on Mr Harris, his voice catching on his words, such was the extent of his rage. 'The Queen is a *b-b-b-beautiful* woman who does not have a *f-f-f-f-fish* face.' Everyone almost lost it again with that one. We, of course, were all in on the private joke that it was our dear Mr Harris who really had the fish face.

We all filed out, and Artie, Holly and I found a quiet corner to talk.

'Well, that backfired. Don't provoke him again, Spike, or he'll expel us all,' warned Holly.

'You worry too much,' I said.

'*You* don't worry enough,' countered Holly.

Artie wasn't listening. 'He's such an idiot,' he said. 'It was just a bit of fun; he didn't need to double our homework. I hate him.'

As we walked back to class, something occurred to me: I should've been scared. But I wasn't. I was having the time of my life. I was enjoying the new power I had as Radio Boy.

You want a fight, Mr Harris? Well, you've got it.

CHAPTER 22

An angry Monkey

I decided it was time to do some more show marketing. Holly was a bit nervous about it at first, but I reminded her there was no way Mr Harris could trace us. Our voices were disguised. And we had the perfect cover thanks to Mr Taggart's 'AV Club lessons'. It was obvious the show was going out live and, as far as Mr Harris knew, we were in class when it did.

For the extra promotion, we decided on flyers

around school in the toilets. Why the toilets? Less chance of teachers seeing them and removing them. Holly, who warmed to the idea quickly since it involved logistics, which is a big thing in the army, suggested that along with our flyers we should also have a photocopy of the newspaper article about Radio Boy.

However, somehow the flyers and article made their way to Mr Harris. He decided the best way to handle this was by having a nuclear meltdown live on Merit Radio.

The speakers actually shook, such was the force of his fury.

In the dining hall, listening, Artie and I smiled at each other. Holly gave us an annoyed look.

'MAYBE I WAS TOO NICE IN MY ASSEMBLY. MY OFFER TO THIS RADIO . . . BOY WAS NOT HEARD OR RESPONDED TO.

'LET ME TELL YOU RIGHT NOW. THERE ARE PEOPLE IN THIS LIFE WHO WILL

AMOUNT TO NOTHING AND BECOME NOBODIES. THOSE ARE THE PEOPLE SOME OF YOU MISGUIDED PUPILS THINK IT'S COOL TO LISTEN TO ON THIS *I-I-I-I—*'

'SPIT IT OUT, FISH FACE!' shouted Artie, earning him huge laughter. Since the secret show had launched, Fish Face was starting to develop a stutter.

'. . . *I-I-I-I-I-I-I-I-I-I-I-I-I-I-I-I-I-I-I-I-I-I-I-I-I-I-I-I-I-I-I-I-I-I-I-I-I-I-I-I-I-ILLEGAL* RADIO BROADCAST. IN A MISERABLE SHED. THEY ARE JEALOUS OF THE GREAT STATION WE HAVE HERE AT MERIT RADIO. THESE PEOPLE ARE SAD AND DESPERATE AND, BY LISTENING TO THEM AND THAT NOISE, YOU ARE ENCOURAGING THEM AND ROTTING YOUR BRAINS. PLEASE STOP.

'THERE WILL BE NO RIVAL TO MERIT RADIO ON MY WATCH.

'*M-M-M-M-M-M-MARK* MY WORDS . . .

THE PUPILS RESPONSIBLE FOR THIS VERBAL VANDALISM WILL BE FOUND, THE STATION WILL BE CLOSED AND THEIR NONSENSE ENDED.

'FOR THE RECORD, I HAVE MY PEOPLE ACTIVELY LOOKING FOR THESE . . . RADIO TERRORISTS.'

Terrorists, were we now?

I could only guess how red that big fish face was. He tried to calm himself as he finished his rant, which I am reflecting here by dropping the ALL CAPITALS of his previous shouting.

'*This . . . this . . . this . . .* is what we do here on Merit Radio. We let our talented pupils' achievements shine. Take Alan Hanson from Year Seven: he is here to treat us to a wonderful recital on his xylophone . . . Alan, work your magic for us . . .'

Alan must've really felt under pressure, as it sounded like he was falling down the stairs with his xylophone.

To say Fish Face's ridiculous rant had really annoyed me was a huge understatement. Nothing we were doing was 'illegal'. Part of me – a big part – really wanted to push him even more. To see how far he could lose it. Luckily, it was Wednesday, which meant I had the perfect chance to voice my right to reply on the show that night.

Before we started the show, Artie and Holly, seeing how amped up I was, tried to talk me down.

'Don't let him get to you – you can't talk about what he said,' pleaded Holly. 'Seriously, this is going to go wrong. I can just feel it.'

'Spike, he's on the edge,' said Artie. 'I mean, it was funny at first, but . . . you heard the stuttering and shouting. Don't make him any worse. We've had our fun, let's just leave it now, yeah?'

I ignored them both. Spike would've been scared, but Radio Boy didn't need to be.

I opened my mic at the start of the show.

'So, we all heard Fish Face shouting about us. Ranting like some bully. Thanks for the plug, Mr Harris. Nice one. Well, in the spirit of helping each other out, I have on the line now Martin Harris, the host of Merit Radio and captain of almost all the sports teams at St Brenda's . . . Martin, thanks for coming on, and no hard feelings . . .'

Artie and Holly looked at each other, worried.

I selected my sound effects. Imagine the sound of an excitable monkey – that's the sound effect I played for Martin Harris talking. Funny, right?

'Well,' I said. 'Martin. What's on Merit Radio tomorrow, Marty?'

The sound of a monkey howling, screaming and jabbering.

'Sounds great, Martin. What are you up to tonight?'

Using sound effects, I made a noise as if a chimp was banging around some saucepans.

'Oh, banging some pans around. Lovely, Martin, that's how you relax, I guess. Well, bye, Martin, thanks for joining us.'

We played a song. The silence in the studio was finally broken by Holly.

'I think you went too far there, Spike,' she said.

She turned the laptop to face me.

A new comment had appeared at the top of the page.

YOU IDIOTS. THIS IS NOW WAR AND YOU WON'T WIN. I WILL MAKE IT MY MISSION IN LIFE TO FIND OUT WHO YOU ARE. YOU CAN'T HIDE FROM ME FOREVER.

It was from a new listener.

Martin Harris.

CHAPTER 23

In

'You went too far, Spike!' Artie shouted, while music played and the mics were off. I'd never heard him shout before.

'I'm not scared of Martin any more. I'll show him.'

'Well, *I'm* scared of him,' said Artie. 'On sports day during the shot-put he threw the shot over the school. That's who's coming after us now – as if it wasn't bad enough that you've already got his dad searching for us. You've turned a whole family against us.'

'And if they find us then what exactly? We aren't actually doing anything wrong. We're untouchable now – we're in the newspaper,' I said.

The current song was coming to an end, and we had a caller on the line. On that night's show we'd been running a phone-in called 'Worst Things About School'.

'Just take it easy, Spike; things are getting a bit crazy. Craig is on the line,' said Holly.

'Hi, it's the *Secret Shed Show* live every Wednesday night. I'm your host, Radio Boy, and on the line now is Craig.'

'Hey, Radio Boy. I think Martin Harris is going to turn the school upside down looking for you now!'

'He won't stop the show, ever,' I assured him. 'Anyway, Craig, what's the worst thing about school for you?'

'Homework. We already get more of it than any other school around here because Mr Harris is so obsessed with grades,' Craig moaned. 'And now he's doubled it!'

'I hear you,' I said. 'The number-one thing everyone has said today on the show is the crazy amount of homework we get. Every show we do it comes up.' I smiled, remembering the Queen homework game.

'It's never going to stop though,' complained caller Craig.

It was right there and then that an idea hit me square in the face. I had been watching the news on TV earlier and it had planted a seed, and now that seed grew into something beautiful . . .

'We should rise up!' I said. 'All the *Secret Shed Show* army of fans must go ON STRIKE!'

'WHAT?' Artie spluttered, sitting bolt upright. He was burning a hole in my head with his angry stare. The owl boy looked ready to pounce on me. I didn't even look over at Holly: the Army Cadet in her would describe this behaviour as 'insubordination', I think.

The news on TV had featured workers at a factory on strike, trying to get a better pay deal. As the strike was on the news and got the factory bad publicity, the management had ended up giving in: it had worked.

'Craig,' I went on. 'If we went on strike to make our voices heard, they would have to listen to how we felt. Could I count on you to strike, Craig, when the moment came?'

'Um, what would we actually do?' Craig didn't sound too convinced.

But I was. Radio Boy to the rescue.

'After lunch break, we all just march out into the playground and sit down. Just sit down. When we're asked what we're doing, we say we're protesting about having too much homework.'

'Won't we get in trouble? Detention?'

Not an unreasonable question from Elvis.

'So what? They really gonna put thirty or forty of us in detention? At least we'll have made a point. Come on, who's with me? Who's had enough of homework?'

I was really getting into this now. I thought about the newspaper article, the Radio Boy graffiti and Fish Face's speech. It all spurred me on.

After a long pause . . .

A really long pause . . .

'I'm in!' said Craig.

'Here's the thing,' I said. 'If we get a hundred of you saying you're in then we'll do it. If not then we'll forget it and decide we aren't serious about having too much homework. This is our chance. So you have this next song to decide. Email me, leave a comment and let me know: are you with me?'

The next song was bang on. 'Anarchy in the UK' by the Sex Pistols. I secretly looked up what anarchy meant on my phone.

'A group of people or a single person rejecting authority.'

Yep, that was about right.

'Guys, you better come see this,' urged Holly, looking at the laptop.

Our eyes were met with a huge amount of new comments coming in every second.

🔘 In

🔘 In

🔘 In

🔘 In

🔘 In

🔘 In

🔘 Do it

🔘 In

🔘 In

🔘 In

🔘 In

🔘 In

In, do it

Strike

Go, Radio Boy

In

In

In

Emails and texts of support continued to pour in until we had over two hundred. Holly and Artie both tried to speak at the same time, I'm guessing to urge me not to do what I was about to do, but the song ended, preventing them.

After a few seconds' silence, I leant closer to the mic.

'You have spoken. Prepare to rise up and strike, followers of the *Secret Shed Show*,' I solemnly declared. 'We will occupy the playground in two days' time. There will be a special extra show tomorrow night to prepare everything. Speak then.'

I signed off.

As Artie looked at me, I could see in his eyes what I was thinking too: this was big.

'What have you done, Spike?' he said. 'You could ruin everything for all of us.'

'Well, that's positive, thanks, Artie,' I said.

'Seriously, Spike,' said Holly. 'What have you done? This isn't what I signed up for: we're going to get EXPELLED, YOU IDIOT.'

'Just keep the faith,' I protested.

I would show them. When we ended up getting less homework, they would be saying *well done* and it would be high fives all round. Which would be nice. Especially since, as we left the shed, my two best friends were looking really angry with me. Neither of them spoke to me. Artie didn't even offer me a stale cake or bun.

CHAPTER 24

No singing chipmunks

I'm going to write this next bit, which happened the following evening, as a movie script. Two reasons:

1. My Hollywood career as a stuntman doesn't look too good after the karate underpants episode (unless there's a major blockbuster about a poor kid and his overbearing, paranoid mum who makes him join various clubs, in

which case I'm the go-to stunt kid for that role). So maybe writing movies might be an easier option for me. You sit in a big chair, yelling at the actors, go to movie festivals in sunny places and appear on TV chat shows with some funny story about the time on set a pigeon pooped on the leading actress's face during a romantic scene. Easy.

2. The three of us sneaking into a shed and broadcasting to the world and leading a homework rebellion (good name for a band, Homework Rebellion) was all starting to feel very much like something from a movie. Of course, definitely a much better movie than the ones my mum makes us watch about talking racoons and singing chipmunks. Before we're allowed to see any film, Mum needs to pre-authorise it, which involves painstaking and time-consuming research

(chatting to other mums) about its content in case we're exposed to anything which could traumatise us FOREVER. It's only recently, since I started at secondary school, that she granted Harry Potter a 'W' certificate (W=Watch).

I think she has access to some hidden part of the internet where 'Mumipedia' lives. An encyclopedia of shared mum 'knowledge'. This details everything that any child could innocently enjoy, but from the unique perspective of a safety-obsessed mother who is a nurse and can SEE DANGER EVERYWHERE.

Mumipedia would look like this for Harry Potter:

This article is about the films with the main character Harry Potter, based on the seven novels in the series.

Harry Potter

Where do I begin? Would you let your little puppykins go to a school with an alcoholic caretaker? Where they study no maths or English BUT ONLY DEVIL POTIONS?

At one point a poor unicorn is SLAUGHTERED and its blood is drunk. Aren't unicorns an endangered species? More importantly, good luck with your kids' nightmares after this dark arts movie.

I will let my son watch this when he is twenty-one and in the company of a priest.

Anyway, for those two reasons, here is the next bit of the story, as a film script.

You should imagine my voice very deep and masterful as you read this. Holly and Artie, meanwhile, sound high-pitched and wimpy.

RADIO BOY THE MOVIE –
A MOVIE WITH NO SINGING CHIPMUNKS
BY
SPIKE HUGHES

Int. Spike's shed – evening.
RADIO BOY *is having a very tense meeting*
with HOLLY *and* ARTIE *minutes before*
that night's radio show.

RADIO BOY *is trying very hard to convince the others that going along with the strike is the right thing to do. RADIO BOY's dark shiny hair looks great and his nose is slightly smaller than in real life in this movie. His teeth are neater and whiter too.*

RADIO BOY

I need you guys to trust me on this. This is our moment to actually do something. This has to happen now or we're letting everyone down.

ELVIS/ARTIE

But we could get into serious trouble . . . expelled. That happens and I bring shame to the family cake empire and I will be sent to some faraway boarding school-type prison where they serve porridge made from cat vomit for breakfast and I'll have my head shoved down the toilet every morning and get a wedgie every day.

HOLLY has been patiently waiting to speak.

HOLLY

Spike, this isn't what we set out to do when we decided to make our own radio show for our friends. We are going to get in real serious trouble that not even I, the highest ranked officer in my Army Cadets, can get us out of. Worst of all for you, Spike, it will be the end of the Secret Shed Show and all this fun. You want Mr Harris and his son tracking us down and murdering us with shot-put balls and bad breath?

NOTE TO DIRECTOR. GET THE ACTRESS PLAYING HOLLY TO WAVE HER HANDS AROUND THE SHED STUDIO WHEN SHE SAYS 'ALL THIS'. THANKS!

RADIO BOY cannot believe they are so worried. They are going to be heroes for once. Why can't they have that just for one day?

RADIO BOY

It's going to be FINE! They can't expel hundreds of us. We can be the ones to finally put a stop to all the homework misery! This will turn us into instant legends! Loved forever around the world as modern heroes, studied in history lessons. Maybe even a bronze statue erected in town and dedicated to me, the unknown rebel leader, RADIO BOY. Maybe in Mexico around campfires they will swap late-night stories of the one they call 'El Radio Boy'.

Extreme close-up on RADIO BOY's *eyes, which have tears in them such is his burning passion.*

RADIO BOY - CONT.
Did you hear Martin Harris talking by the sports lockers today?

(RADIO BOY *knows that will motivate his team: their shared hatred of the headmaster's son and presenter of* MERIT RADIO, MARTIN HARRIS. *In the movie,* MARTIN HARRIS *will be way uglier than in actual real life. I would even suggest casting someone like a tramp to play him.*)

HOLLY
What did he say, Spike?

ELVIS

Guy's a total idiot times, like, a million.

Extreme close-up of RADIO BOY's *face as he winks to the camera. As if saying TOLD YOU SO to the audience.*

RADIO BOY

I heard him and one of the other apes talking about our radio show, and the strike. Martin actually said it's just 'nerds talking big' who won't go through with it - that's what his dad Fish Face told him. And that no one will join us. Easy to be brave in a website comment, but in real life it's a joke. That's what they said.

ELVIS and HOLLY look really annoyed. HOLLY's ears, which are very visible to the eye due to the sharp angle they are positioned on her head, glow bright red. A sure sign she is angry.

RADIO BOY – CONT.
Plus, I have a great back-up plan. You need to trust me on this.

HOLLY and ELVIS (TOGETHER)
What?

RADIO BOY
You'll see . . . Holly, when I hand you a phone number during tonight's show, just call it live and put them on air so we can all hear the call.

Scene ends with me (RADIO BOY) grinning. Is doing a thumbs-up at the camera too much?

CHAPTER 25

A brilliant mistake I'm about to make

Time to move from Hollywood back to Crow Crescent and that evening's strike countdown show. This was an extra show, a bonus one, to make sure the listeners were ready to launch S-DAY (Strike Day) the following lunchtime.

I double-checked and then triple-checked that the voice disguiser was ready to go, then opened the mics. The bright red glow of the MIC LIVE sign seemed to shine even brighter tonight as if it wanted me to know it believed in me.

'Good evening, this is the *Secret Shed Show* and tonight's show is a Strike Special because tomorrow is the big day when we get our chance to show them what we're made of.

'They don't think we're going to go through with it. We must. They think we're all nerds who just talk. Not my words but the words of our headmaster, Fish Face, and his puppet fish son. But we are not just talk. We are people of action. And there are too many of us to ignore. Let's just remind ourselves why we're doing this.'

I played tonight's first song. 'No More Homework' by someone called Gary U.S. Bonds. Perfect. Where on earth did Artie find these records? Written in olden times when everything was black and white, back in 1963. Decades later, homework was still ruining kids' lives.

But not any more.

The song faded to its end.

'. . . Radio Boy here. That song sums it all up. Tomorrow we strike. I know you are all getting a bit scared. Even rock-steady Elvis is worried about getting a detention or expelled. But we have a right to strike. Mr Harris can't expel hundreds of us or he'll have no one to shout at! He *lives* to yell and shout at us – we all know that. I think he was born yelling at the midwife and his mum. Believe me: we will be remembered by history for what we are about to do. People will sing songs about us.'

I was getting into this. You might even say I was getting a bit carried away with it all. Would the old me, Spike Hughes, have done this? Probably not.

But Radio Boy could. I stood up to carry on with my rousing speech to my fellow rebels on air.

'RISE UP, EVERYONE . . . BUT ERM . . . SIT DOWN IN THE PLAYGROUND. THE RISE UP MEANS IN . . . ERM . . . SPIRIT. YOU CAN RISE UP, BUT STILL BE SITTING DOWN.'

'Don't think you can actually,' Elvis chipped in, unhelpfully.

'Anyway, I need to make a very important call right now, live on air,' I announced. I sat back down dramatically and handed Holly a piece of paper with a phone number on it.

'Just call that number, my Secret Shed Producer, please?' I asked Holly on air. Begrudgingly, she did.

She put the call through to me so everyone listening could hear me take it live on air. Like Howard 'The Howie' Wright did on his breakfast show when they called a competition winner.

Time for my back-up plan that would *really* get us noticed when we went on strike. Trust me, old Mr Harris would be stunned at this move. In chess, I think it's known as a checkmate.

We all heard the phone ringing live on the show. No one listening, or in the shed, knew what I was up to.

Then a voice answered. 'Hello?'

CHAPTER 26

captain Invisible Nerd

'Hello,' I said. 'Is that the *Gazette* news desk?'

'Yes, it is,' said the voice.

'Say hi to everyone listening.'

'Er . . . hi.'

'To whom do I have the pleasure of speaking?'

This was something I'd heard my mum say once.

'I'm Derek Mountfield, news editor,' said the voice on the phone, suspiciously. 'And I'd like to know what—'

'Then it's you I want to speak to, Mr Mountfield! You wrote an article about me and my *Secret Shed Show*.'

'Ah!' said the voice, friendlier now. 'The infamous RADIO BOY! We meet at last.'

'Yes, it's me, Derek, if I may call you Derek?'

'Sure.'

'Thanks, Derek. You're on the air and I'm giving you my first ever exclusive interview. I have something to say. Do you have a pen?'

'Right . . . no . . . gimme a second to grab my pad.' Derek the newsman sounded excited. He was getting a MAJOR local news exclusive – maybe of the year or of his career. Must have felt good taking a break from reporting on vandals spray-painting a pensioner or the mayor opening a new youth centre.

'Ready, Radio Boy. What do you want to say?'

'Come down to St Brenda's school tomorrow at 1pm to see history made,' I said.

'Well, what an offer. At the moment, let me check my diary . . . oh, the mayor is opening a new rubbish tip, but maybe I could cover your story if it's bigger. What's happening at 1pm?'

'The kids at St Brenda's are going on STRIKE! Hundreds of us.'

'Kids? Striking!? Wow! That *is* more interesting than the opening of the new rubbish tip. I'll ditch the mayor for you, Radio Boy.'

We could hear him making notes excitedly. Time for another great question from the news hound.

'So what exactly are you striking about, Radio Boy?' asked Derek. 'Let me guess . . . Standard of the dinner ladies' food? Can't use Snapchat during lessons?'

'Homework,' I replied.

'Homework?' I may have been wrong, but I think I heard newsman Derek try to stifle a giggle.

'Yes! We are doing too much and Derek, you

can quote me on this. WE ARE NOT GOING TO TAKE IT ANY MORE.'

I hit my hand on the desk for extra effect, and a few plant pots fell off a shed shelf. Without even saying goodbye to Derek Mountfield, I went straight into the next song. And what a song. 'We're Not Gonna Take It' by a terrifying-looking group called Twisted Sister. This was our strike anthem. The Queen has her anthem, and I had mine, sung by grown men wearing make-up.

I thought Artie and Holly would be impressed by my genius masterplan. Derek Mountfield, coming to witness history and report on it, putting even more pressure on the school to change its ways. It was clear, however, that they *weren't* impressed. They couldn't even look at me. For the first time in our friendship, it seemed they didn't know what to say to me.

Why couldn't they see we were at a crossroads: to stay put as lifelong members of the walking prey at school or to rise up and strike?

Holly spoke up first.

'I'm not sure I'll be with you tomorrow, Spike.'

'I definitely won't be. Not sure who you are any more. Spike, or Radio Boy,' said Artie.

'Well, thanks, Artie!' I said. 'Some best mate. So you'd rather we just run away back home now and stop it all and carry on as we were? Go back to being invisible and just enjoy Merit Radio. Well, I want more and—'

'That's not what we're saying, Spike!' said Holly. 'You've got the local paper coming now. That's going to push Mr Harris totally over the edge like we've never seen before. You want to carry on making this huge mistake? Then you can do it without us. What's happened to you, Spike? You've changed. And not in a nice way.'

Holly stung me with that one. Was I really changing? Yes, but for the good, right? Not hiding and scared any more. I'd started the radio show wanting to change something, but it had also changed me. I felt like I'd been sleepwalking for most of my life and now I'd finally woken up. At long last I'd found out what it was like to be captain of the school football team or karate champion. I didn't want to go back to being just Spike Hughes, Captain Invisible Nerd of the AV Club. I felt important and powerful for the first time in my life.

'You are going to be there really, aren't you?' I asked Holly and Artie.

Nothing. Neither of them said anything.

CHAPTER 27

Oh very No

I didn't sleep very well that night. Constantly thinking about what I should have said that would have made Artie and Holly see how important the strike was. And at the same time turning over and over in my mind how I could make the strike even bigger.

When I woke up, it came to me.

They say time can slow down, and I never knew what that really meant until Friday's S-DAY.

Lunch break dragged on endlessly, limping its way towards the time for action. That's if anyone really did join me in the planned sit-down protest. I kept looking at my watch and I spotted a few other kids doing the same. Like some secret sign that they too were part of the resistance.

Some were in groups, talking excitedly. I detected a growing buzz about what was about to happen.

Blissfully unaware of the excitement in the dinner hall was Merit Radio, which carried on in its usual badness. I heard only a few select sound bites as my mind was on the approaching showdown, but I think I heard one of St Brenda's pupils doing the alphabet backwards to great fake applause in the studio.

Now it was time to put my plan into action.

I snuck away from the main hall and made my way to the headmaster's office. It really should have been an aquarium as that would be the perfect home for Fish Face. I knew he would be in the staffroom during lunch break, holding court while devouring a sausage roll the size of his head. As you know, Mr Harris loves sausage rolls. As a result, the Sausage Jumbo is one of Mr Cake's bestsellers. I think sales from Fish Face's addiction to them paid for Artie's house. Every afternoon, if you had the misfortune of seeing Mr Harris, there would be bits of sausage roll on his suit jacket and tie. Like he had pastry dandruff.

So: there would be no problem with Mr Harris. I just had to get past his secretary, Mrs Hubert. She sometimes hangs around at her desk just outside his office during the lunch break, working through her hour off to type up Fish Face's latest angry letter to some poor parent about their underperforming kid. She's like his terrified pet. Always trying to keep bad news from getting to him for fear of a Fish Face spit explosion.

I casually walked towards Mrs Hubert's desk,

outside the gates of hell – mentally preparing some kind of excuse for my presence. But . . . she wasn't there. Result! The coast was clear; maybe she had finally run away to join the circus. Would we see her on the evening news?

'*Good evening. Breaking news tonight of a school secretary who has disappeared. Mrs Hubert, 59, who works for the devil, was last seen wearing a sparkly leotard in the company of a Bulgarian trapeze artist named Radko.*'

It looked like the day was going to go my way. I doubled back and slid for the first time ever into the belly of the beast. Mr Harris's office.

It took me a few moments to take in the spectacle before me. I'm not making this up when I say all his walls were covered in pictures of himself apart from one of the Queen of England. Behind his office chair was a huge painting of himself!

Whoever'd had the misfortune of being hired

to do this portrait of the monster must have been reduced to a quivering mess, having to sit a few metres away from such a hideous beast. Mr Harris looked like a jumbo sausage that had been left too long on one of my dad's barbecues. Ready to burst.

Then there was the smell. *An animal must have died in here,* I thought. It smelled of sweating cows and beefy burps. How could anyone work in such an environment?

I left the letter I had prepared earlier on his desk and got out quickly, for fear of collapsing from the sickening stench.

It was just minutes away from the end of lunch break. My palms were getting sweaty.

If I'm honest, I was scared and worried that no one would go through with the strike. I would be like a leader whose army had deserted him.

But as I came back into the main hall an amazing sight awaited me. Groups of kids were heading out, excitedly. I joined them at the back.

As we all got to the playground, the excitement evaporated and fear took its place. Everyone was cautiously hanging around the edges, waiting for someone else to go and sit down first.

Did it need to be me? What if no one joined in? Would my cover be broken as Radio Boy?

Giles Hunter, the new kid, was the first to break ranks and head out into the middle of the playground. I recognised a few of the others who joined him. They had been callers and emailers to the show! I recognised Craig from Year 8, Lotty, Tom, Alex. Our loyal fans!

I only wondered . . . would Artie and Holly come? I felt bad about the way we'd left things. Like something important was missing. We had started this adventure together and created this amazing moment; it didn't seem right for us all not to share in it.

Heart racing, I went to join the strikers. As Spike Hughes on the outside, but as Radio Boy on the inside. There were lines of kids heading towards us. I reckoned there were now over a hundred of us. Sitting down. Protesting. All because a secret radio show in a shed on Crow Crescent had told

them to. My heart was pounding. I had never felt so much adrenaline in me before. It was like I'd eaten ten of Artie's sugar-coated doughnuts.

It didn't take long for the strike to have an effect.

First out was Mrs Hubert – clearly, she hadn't run away. The expression on her face made me feel a bit guilty actually. She's a kind, decent woman (with a cat face), and she could sense something was happening and that her boss wasn't going to like it.

'Now come on, everyone, back to class,' she said, anxiously. 'Is this the Radio Boy thing? Oh, come on before you get in trouble . . .'

Her reasoned pleas fell on deaf ears.

'PLEEEEAAASE,' was her next effort, even folding her hands together while she said it, as if intoning a prayer.

Still nothing.

Sighing, she trotted off to get reinforcements.

A few moments later, she returned with a

reinforcement, in the form of the head of sport, Mr Jackson. A fearsome man. I almost admired her plan: she was unleashing the school guard dog before Mr Harris knew anything about it.

Mr Jackson's hair is always perfect, like the men who model shorts in Mum's clothing catalogue. For some reason, they are always on a yacht, pointing to something on the horizon. That's what Mr Jackson looks like. Mr Catalogue Man. ALWAYS wearing shorts, regardless of the weather. He doesn't have mere human skin, he has weatherproof skin like a bin bag.

He also has a *very* loud voice.

'GET BACK TO YOUR CLASSROOMS NOW!!!!' he shouted.

He bellowed so loudly that schoolchildren in Africa would have heard him and sprinted back to their classrooms. But today, for the first time in St Brenda's school history, his words didn't have their normal power.

In fact, they had the opposite effect. They made us more defiant.

One of us yelled back at him: 'NO MORE HOMEWORK!'

Mr Jackson was a talented sportsman in his youth, playing for the England under-16s football team, and only a bad tackle ended his promising career. Which is to say, fair play and team spirit are important to him. He shouts about them often enough when drilling us in football techniques (I mean, failing to teach me football techniques). As a result, he seemed quietly impressed with the spirit and heart of the reply and our protest.

Nevertheless, he still fired back, ever the sportsman trying to win the challenge.

'GET UP!'

No one did.

'NO MORE HOMEWORK!' several voices yelled back at the same time. Then more, including me, joined in.

'NO MORE HOMEWORK! NO MORE HOMEWORK! NO MORE HOMEWORK!'

Hundreds of us were now chanting together. All as one voice. I was shaking with the excitement of what was happening, and the unknown of what was going to happen next.

Mr Jackson and Mrs Hubert chatted together intensely – it looked like Mrs Hubert was bringing our sports teacher up to speed with the *Secret Shed Show*, Radio Boy and this strike. Then there was a very strange noise that none of us, not the kids striking nor Mr Jackson and Mrs Hubert, will ever forget for the rest of our lives. I imagine it will remain a shared experience, so that if any of us bump into one another in twenty or thirty years' time, we'll look at each other and, without needing to say a single word, just *know* we heard that noise.

It was a noise like no other. It was part war cry

and part human grown man, crying and yelling at the same time. I think it's what hell must sound like. I'll try to recapture it here for you:

'*ARGHGHHGHGHGHGHGYIP*—
WHATTHEHELL—
ARGGHHHHHHHHHHHHHHHH—
IN ALL MY YEARS SEEN SUCH—
NOOOO—
RADIO BOYYYYYYYYYYYYYYYYY!'

Mr Harris was no longer Fish Face. He had the face of an angry, barking dog that had broken free of its lead and wanted to bite somebody.

No. I've got it! He was a human volcano, exploding forth all the rage that had been lying dormant in him. (*Can you tell we'd just been doing volcanoes in geography? No other way would I ever use the word 'dormant'. That word is linked with volcanoes for life. You wouldn't use it in any other context. 'This morning I had some pizza that had been lying dormant in the fridge.'*

'My dad had been sitting dormant on the couch for an hour.')

In Mr Harris's hand, which was clenched in an angry fist, was the piece of paper I'd left on his desk.

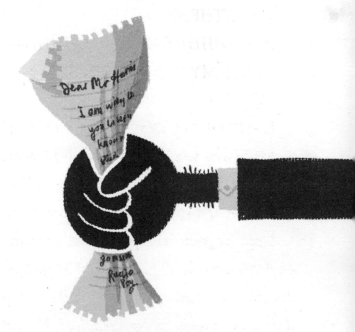

Mr Harris stopped spewing his molten lava (*you see why I got a B for my volcano project*) and took in the sea of striking kids. He stood eerily still. Silence fell over the playground.

A silence broken a moment later by the unmistakable sound of a helicopter overhead. It was so low you could read the letters on its undercarriage:

Derek the reporter must have realised this was the story of the year and told his fellow reporters on the TV news team. We were going to be an item on the news that night!

We saw it. Mr Harris saw it and his shoulders sank, like someone getting really bad news. Moments passed and then something even more terrifying happened.

He started smiling.

He waved my cleverly disguised demand note in the air at us.

'So, you want less homework? Radio Boy has got you all to do this. Impressive. I even appreciate the organisation that has gone into it – if only you could channel those energies into your schoolwork. But it all ends now with this important announcement . . .'

Mrs Hubert got ready with her pen and pad. As did Derek the reporter, who had appeared at some point and was now standing next to her.

Mr Jackson flexed his muscles in his way-too-short satin sports shorts.

'If I don't find Radio Boy, I will keep your homework doubled FOR A YEAR.' He paused. 'However, I am prepared to be generous. The first person who brings me the name, the true identity of Radio Boy, gets NO HOMEWORK FOR THE REST OF THEIR TIME AT ST BRENDA'S!'

Oh no.

Oh very no.

CHAPTER 28

The most wanted boy in the school

So many thoughts were racing around my head.

- I've got Mr Harris cornered.
- I'm winning.
- There's a HELICOPTER reporting on us!
- HELICOPTER!
- Radio Boy, me, Spike Hughes, did all this.
- I've got my own gang, my listeners.

- I've never been part of a gang.
- And I'm NOT ANY MORE.
- Within a few moments, the tables have been turned.
- Fish Face is back in control.
- I'm now being HUNTED by my own listeners.
- He's put a bounty on my head.
- I'm the most wanted boy in the school.
- You can escape from the police anywhere, but not from your own school.
- Who can I trust?
- Did they just say my name?
- Can I trust Artie and Holly?
- The bounty on my head is HUGE.
- No homework FOREVER?
- You even know what a 'bounty' is? 'Reward for capturing a fugitive.'
- I'm a FUGITIVE?
- Does this make me more/less attractive to Katherine Hamilton?

- Do women marry FUGITIVES?
- Do I need to go on the run?
- Did I feed Sherlock this morning?

CHAPTER 29

Diary of a fugitive

Well, I guess, on the plus side, the Hollywood movie of my life had just got way more exciting.

It was no longer just a movie about a kid with a secret radio show live from a shed who decides to take on the world.*

It was now a sure-fire box office smash hit about a kid FUGITIVE. The world's most wanted boy. An outlaw. A masked crusader, adored by many, feared by many more.

* By 'world' I mean the headmaster, but to a kid that is the world.

Most of my dad's action movies that Mum has permitted me to watch have a manhunt in them. This seems to involve a lot of running around, panting heavily, sweating and looking over your shoulder all the time. Some require you to leap into a raging river below. I hope this bit doesn't happen to me as I can only do a half-decent front crawl and my mum would go berserk if I did any river jumping within an hour of eating a heavy meal.

If I have to go on the run from Mr Harris and leave my family home in Crow Crescent then I will take my dog Sherlock with me. No way could I leave him behind.

BUT have you ever seen a movie about a fugitive kid and his DOG? Not sure how to cast the role of Sherlock in the movie. How good are dog actors? Would they respond to direction or just lie on the floor having a nap during a key scene?

Maybe this is why they don't have awards at the Oscars for Best Animal Actor in a movie. Just getting the winning cat, pony, dolphin or dog up on stage would be hard, let alone getting a speech out of them. There is also the risk the dog might lift its leg live on TV and take a pee against the award host's podium.

Anyway. Fish Face, I have to admit, had played a very clever move that I never saw coming. I'd underestimated his fishy ways. Mr Harris had outsmarted me. No homework for the rest of their time at the school, in return for giving up Radio Boy's identity.

Killer move.

Who wouldn't search high and low for me with that amazing prize up for grabs? Fish Face could just sit back on his throne in his honking office, stuffing his face with jumbo sausage rolls, and wait for the tip-off to come in.

Except . . . he didn't just do that.

That afternoon, after the playground strike reached its premature and frustrating conclusion, I was trying to get used to my new fugitive status. Not so much escaping fleeing dogs tracking me by jumping into a river canyon, just a really boring double maths lesson. As I worked, I was attempting to ignore the constant murmur of gossip speculating about who Radio Boy might be, and the worrying rumours about Mr Harris's investigation.

Fish Face was in his element and could smell victory – well, that or another animal had died in his office. He had now converted his stinking, beefy headquarters into a temporary interrogation room. Judging by the reports from the unlucky kids who'd been taken in for questioning by the school prefects, the interrogation room consisted of:

- A bright light shining into your face to

intimidate you (from the drama department, covered in glitter from the recent *Joseph* production, so not that scary).

- Mr Harris with no jacket on and his sleeves rolled up, revealing the hairiest arms in the world. Even a gorilla would think he needed a trim. Yet more evidence that Martin Harris really is an ape-child.

- The blood pressure pumpy thing from the school nurse, to measure any sudden rise in your anxiety levels. A makeshift lie detector to indicate whether you might be harbouring the identity of Radio Boy.

- Poor Mrs Hubert making notes like a cat-faced detective and wishing she had decided to run away and join the circus.

The prefects had become Mr Harris's prison guards, and the innocent suspects were marched one by one to the interrogation chamber from their classes. When they returned, many of them appeared to have been crying and several may actually have wet themselves.

Artie and Holly cornered me.

'What you gonna do, Spike? We warned you,' whispered Artie.

'You HAVE to turn yourself in – this is awful,' hissed Holly.

'Look, this will blow over by the end of today and by Monday, after a weekend of getting nowhere, he'll calm down. If you don't say anything, it will just blow over. Trust me.'

The question was: could I trust them? Would they turn me in to get a lifetime off homework?

I hoped not. I really hoped not.

I was about to ask them, but then . . .

At that very moment all three of us looked down the corridor to see Nick Culverwell and Josh Jones, two of the head prefects/prison guards, approaching with Martin Harris.

'Come on then, weirdos, let's go,' Martin said, and his hench-apes stared at us as if we were dirt. It was our turn to be 'invited' into the interrogation chamber of horrors. My stomach tightened with fear and I could tell by the throbbing blood vessel bulging out of Artie's forehead that he was scared too. Even tough nut Holly seemed frightened, as her ears had turned a dark shade of scarlet.

Had someone named us already?

Had Mr Taggart come clean about his part in all this in exchange for a pay rise? Everybody has their price.

Holly was tough, but Artie was terrified of being sent to boarding school. They could easily break him. Offer him a doughnut or some cash for new records as a bribe and he would roll on his back and let Mr Harris tickle his belly.

This was bad. As we walked down the corridor, my stomach felt hollow and like it was spinning at the same time.

I was the first in.

I left Artie and Holly to sweat some more outside in the corridor on some especially uncomfortable wooden benches. By the way, why is most of the school seating for kids so awful? Do they buy it from a special warehouse run by a former teacher whose life was made a misery by unruly pupils, so now he gets his own back making painfully uncomfortable school chairs and benches?

Anyway, back to the chamber of torture. I was swiftly ushered into. My eyes took in the sadistic spectacle before them. All the various tools of interrogation I'd heard about were there.

- Eye-burning lights
- Blood pressure lie detector
- Nervy-looking Mrs Hubert

What I hadn't expected to see was that the

huge whiteboard normally used for dull maths equations or chemical formulas now held various photos of pupils in two columns.

'SUSPECTS' and 'NOT THEM'.

When the police do this for a big murder investigation or something, the photos of the criminal suspects are mugshots and look really mean and scary. Mr Harris's board, full of smiling kids' faces from their annual school photos, didn't have quite the same effect. The FBI doesn't issue wanted posters with Cody Vincent from 5b's gap-toothed, smiling face in his school tie and blazer.

More worryingly, the interrogation chamber also contained a detailed satellite map of our town on the wall with pins in it. Red pins and blue pins in various back gardens. It didn't take me long to work out that a blue pin marked a house with a shed. So now we had a shed hunt and a manhunt.

I was trying to find my house when Mr Harris sauntered in, whistling.

He seemed very casual. Was this a ruse? Some mind trick he'd heard the Germans did in the war?

'This won't take long for you, Spike. Same with your fellow AV Club spods.'

There was something about the way he patronisingly said 'AV Club': as if it was a joke. Well, Fish Face, I don't see any joke in studying the multidisciplines of sound and vision.

'Don't look so worried,' he continued. 'I know it can't be *you lot*.'

There he went again. '*You lot*', as if we were barely functioning, spineless bags of organs. I was relieved but annoyed at the same time: almost tempted to confess just to see the surprised look on his face.

Mr Harris chuckled to himself at the very thought that we could build a station in a shed, get equipment, plan a show, carry it off and motivate everyone to strike.

'I mean, your mum would never let such a thing happen, would she?' he went on as I sat there, silent. 'And you a mummy's boy if ever I saw one, eh? *He he he he.*'

More snorting. I don't think I could've hated him any more.

'No, you're only in here so I can fire a few names at you. Remember, I'll give you the rest of your time here off homework if I can find out who this idiot Radio Boy is. No one needs to know you told me – it can be a special secret we share.' The thought of sharing anything with Fish Face made me feel a bit sick.

'No idea, Mr Harris,' I said. 'Trust me, if I knew, I would say.'

'Guessed as much. Right, better chat to the others, Arnie and Dolly.'

'Artie and Holly, sir.'

'Exactly.'

I left his office/interrogation chamber and winked as I walked towards Artie and Holly. Artie looked terrified, Holly chilled. Their prison warden escorts had left them alone. Neither of them really met my eye though.

'Easy!' I said. 'Apparently, we're far too spineless to have done this. He just wants information. Be cool. He didn't even get your names right.'

'I've done counter-interrogation training with the cadets, so he won't break me. Unless I decide I want to tell him,' said Holly.

'You won't, will you?' I said.

She rolled her eyes. Did that mean ... obviously not? I wasn't sure.

A horrible thought occurred to me. If Holly and Artie spilled the beans, our friendship would be over forever. I would officially have no friends. None at all.

At the end of school that day, I waited anxiously for them both outside the school gates. Our normal meeting spot. As everyone filed past, there was still only one thing being discussed: who was Radio Boy and how could they uncover him?

I couldn't see Artie or Holly.

I sent them both texts:

R u ok? Please don't give me up. Radio Boy can fix this.

No replies. Nothing.

Now I was getting really worried. I couldn't help but imagine what kind of fresh interrogation torture they were undergoing. Was Artie being made to endure Abigail Dickins playing the recorder non-stop? The poor kid. Who could blame him if he gave me up?

And actually . . . were they . . . maybe . . . right?

That I had gone too far? I mean, kids being interrogated was not part of my plan.

I dragged myself home full of a thousand different concerns and no one to talk about them with. I got back and managed to pull myself together by bringing Sherlock up to speed with the day's events. He listened intently while drooling as the story took its unexpected twist with my manhunt. After my debrief with Sherlock, I decided action was the best way forward, so I posted on our website and Facebook that there would be a special show that night.

I needed to speak directly to my listeners, friends and enemies alike.

I needed to do what I'd told Holly and Artie I would do.

I needed to fix this.

Meanwhile . . .

What I didn't know, as I spoke to Sherlock, was that Mr Harris had already received information that I was Radio Boy.

Remember Graham, the human gnome from my old hospital radio? The man whose studio I filled with stink bombs and who I got suspended after he almost caught us during the heist?

Turns out his grandson goes to my school. The gnome heard about Radio Boy and the Secret Shed Show, and put two and two together. He wasted no time in phoning up Mr Harris to turn me in.

But I was lucky.

Fish Face checked his satellite map and my address. And . . . he didn't see the shed. Remember me telling you it was all grown over with bushes? Well, they were still there: Dad may have tidied the inside of the shed and the path, but the roof was still completely covered.

Seeing only shrubbery in our garden, Mr Harris ignored Graham the Gnome's tip-off. Those dagger-like thorns turned out to be the thing that kept my identity secret . . . for the time being.

I was safe.

But not for long.

CHAPTER 30

The WORLD's worst apology

I had a plan to fix things, but I also had to do everything I possibly could to try to get Artie and Holly back for that night's show.

I needed them.

Which meant I needed to *talk* to them. To apologise. They were the only friends I had and I'd let them down. I told Dad I was going to be doing a one-off exam revision radio show that night and we needed a cover story as Mum would be at home. He came up with a great idea and told Mum not to worry if she saw me heading to the shed as I was working on a very special present for her birthday.

But later, as I set off to find Artie and Holly, I saw that Dad had more pressing concerns. He was under some intense cross-examination from Mum. Mum made Mr Harris look an amateur at interrogation.

'Can you tell me why several hundred pounds have been spent on eBay items?' she said to him, brandishing a credit-card bill.

Sorry, Dad, forgot to tell you about that . . .

'I . . . I . . . meant to speak to you about that,' he said. 'I . . .'

I could almost see my dad's brain furiously scanning his database for an excuse. He picked a bad one.

'I've been getting some second-hand equipment as I've been thinking about playing the drums again, you know, like in a band or something . . .' he offered.

'WHAT! AT YOUR AGE? AREN'T YOU TOO OLD FOR THAT?'

'Well, no, actually—'

'If it's second-hand equipment, it will be LETHAL! Did I tell you about the poor boy on my ward who got electrocuted by his guitar? FRIED HIS HAND RIGHT OFF!'

'What?'

'All he has now is a small doll's hand they had to attach to him.'

With Mum in full medical horror mode, I snuck out. But not before I saw Dad glaring at me. *Yeah. I did mean to tell you about all that. Sorry again, Dad. Gotta go.*

My bike had a flat tyre, so in desperation to get to Artie and Holly as quickly as I could, I had to borrow Mum's. It was fluorescent pink so as to be visible at night (safety first always with

Mum) and had a big wicker shopping basket on the front. The sight of a boy clearly on his mum's bike, which was also too big for him, was making heads turn as I sped out of Crow Crescent, the pedals a blur.

It didn't take long to reach Artie's house. I hurtled up the crunchy gravel driveway. I saw Holly's bike outside. Great, they were both here.

I rang the bell at Gateaux Chateau: no answer.

I knew they were inside though, and I was pretty sure I saw Artie's owl-like face appear, then quickly disappear, from the front-room window. They were avoiding me. This was all such a mess.

I pushed the huge letter box open and called through. 'Artie, Holly, it's Spike. Please let me in. I know you're there. I need you two.'

Artie's Jack Russell, Douglas, started his usual irritating habit of yapping non-stop.

I peered in through the letter box again.

Me: Hey it's me, come on.

Stupid Dog: YAP YAP YAP YAP.

Me, louder: HOW LONG HAVE WE BEEN FRIENDS?

Stupid Dog, getting even louder too: YAP YAP YAP.

Me, yelling now: YOU ARE MY BEST FRIENDS, PLEASE—

But at this point, not content with ruining my apology with his awful high-pitched yapping, Douglas, the world's most irritating dog, took a huge chunk out of my left hand, which had been propping the letter box open.

'ARGGGHHHH!' I cried out. Not even *this*, my cry of genuine agony, brought either of my friends out to see if I was OK or bleeding to death.

Then Holly broke the silence from an upstairs window that suddenly opened.

'I hope he hurt you! Might bite some sense into you. It's all about you. Not about us. I told you to back off Mr Harris and—'

'I know, I'm so—'

'What about us, Spike? We could be expelled thanks to your BIG HEAD and your dumb strike. We never wanted the show to be secret in the first place. That was YOUR STUPID IDEA.'

The window slammed shut.

I shouted up.

'PLEASE, I'M SORRY! I NEED YOU. JUST ONE MORE SHOW. TONIGHT. I'M GOING TO MAKE IT ALL RIGHT.'

Then Artie started blasting his music at full volume to drown me out. I stood no chance. His speakers were the size of my dad.

As ever, Artie let his music do the talking. He was playing Ugly Kid Joe's 'Everything About You', which if you're not familiar with the lyrics basically goes 'I hate everything about you' about three thousand times.

Subtle, Artie, subtle.

I reached into my backpack, found a pen and

paper and wrote a note:

Artie, ~~Holly~~

I'm really sorry. I messed up big time. Please ~~forgive~~ forgive me.
Meet me at the shed TONIGHT.

Spike

Ps Really SORRY
PPS Good song choice Artie

I was halfway through putting it through the letter box when Douglas grabbed it from my hand and began eating it. Could the day get any worse?

Yes.

It really could.

Meanwhile . . .

What I didn't know then, and only found out later, was that Mr Harris was getting another tip-off.

And this one he didn't disregard.

Guess who it came from?

Yes, that's right – the one person who could BREAK MY HEART by turning me in.

The tip-off came from . . .

Katherine Hamilton. The girl I wanted to marry.

What happened was this: while Holly was being interrogated by Mr Harris, she left her phone back in the classroom.

Katherine Hamilton took it home, thinking that she would give it to Holly the next day. At least that was her story later. Since she turned out to be such a SNAKE, I wouldn't be surprised if she was just helping herself to it.

Anyway, she got home, and put Holly's phone on the table while she made herself some kind of snake snack of mice or whatever witches eat.

Which is when the phone pinged with a message from me.

A message from me to Holly.

THE message in fact I'd sent, saying don't give me up and that Radio Boy could fix this. Then, of course, she saw who the message was from.

Spike Hughes.

My once-future wife picked up her own phone and dialled the school office number. She didn't even hesitate. She gave me up in a heartbeat, in exchange for no more homework.

But what about the overgrown foliage covering our shed?

Well.

Remember when my sister said that Katherine Hamilton had changed since I used to be friends with her in primary school?*

So this is how it went down; it will make your blood boil.

Mr Harris: *Katherine, thank you for the information, but I've already ruled Spike Hughes out of the investigation. He doesn't have a shed, you see.*

Katherine Hamilton (the girl I will now never marry even at gunpoint): *Oh no, Mr Harris, he does. It's just really overgrown. There's, like, brambles all over it.*

Mr Harris: *Really? How do you know?*

Katherine Hamilton: *I used to play round there all the time. It was like a joke in the family, how his dad left all these bushes to grow, and how they covered the shed. They called it the jungle.*

Mr Harris, checking out his satellite map: *Interesting, Katherine. Very interesting.*

Me: *Busted.*

---

* *I've just checked: this was way back in Chapter 5, so I'll forgive you if you forgot. I actually like you more for instantly forgetting anything to do with my older sister.*

CHAPTER 31

The NET closes

That night I could just *sense* Mum's prying eyes behind her bedroom curtains, watching me as I made my way to the shed. In her mind, I'd be crafting, building and painting some amazing gift for her birthday. I would've felt guilty about the deception, or worried about what I *was* going to give her for her birthday, but I didn't have time for that. I was on a mission to protect my identity and save the show.

Being in the shed without Artie and Holly felt really odd. I'd texted them again, saying what I was doing and that I needed them, but still nothing.

Focus, Spike, focus. I put my mind back on the job in hand. The only thing I could control right now was the *Secret Shed Show*. Secret for how much longer though?

I did my normal pre-show checks, like a pilot before take-off. This was the checklist Producer Holly had made for me; just seeing it made me a bit sad.

- Turn on equipment
- Turn on fan to keep equipment cool and us too
- Check phone working
- Log into our website
- Check show messages, emails, texts, message board posts.
- Reply to all of the messages

- Check voice disguiser
- Check headphone levels
- Check microphone levels
- Check song levels
- Write notes on what I want to say
- Check voice disguiser again
- Check Sherlock has water in his bowl

Everything checked and done, I started the show. The song I'd chosen carefully to continue Artie's great work: 'Fight the Power' by Public Enemy.

I opened the mic.

'Radio Boy here. This is the *Secret Shed Show*.'

As I spoke, however, I realised I just didn't feel like Radio Boy, the invisible superhero, any more. My superpowers were fading along with the listeners' faith in me.

'So, I guess we need to talk about today. Firstly, thanks for showing up for the strike. For a few minutes, we did something special. We had a voice, hundreds of us as ONE.'

I wanted the listeners to believe the strike had been worthwhile, despite the bounty on my head, and the now-looming threat of double homework for a year. But I wasn't even sure I believed that myself any more. I was still hoping, however, that my listeners would stand by me.

I could see I had a call on the show mobile so I nervously took it straight on air. I had no idea what they were going to say.

'Hi, Radio Boy here, you're live on air. Who's calling?'

'No, Radio Boy, who are *you*?' said the voice on the line. 'We love this show and what you do, but we've all been dragged into Mr Harris's pit of hell now to be interrogated, giving us nightmares for life, all so *you* can hide?'

'Well . . . I . . .'

I couldn't think of anything to say.

I hung up and took another call.

'Hello, who's this? You're live on the *Secret Shed Show*.' I was hopeful this caller would be more on my side . . .

'Hey, Radio Boy, tell me, why do you need it to be a secret who you really are? Chatting to my mates, we don't care who you are; we love the show. Why do you need to hide? We need you to do the right thing for us. You said you were our friend.'

I hung up. Took another call.

'Hello, line two, you're live on the air,' I lied. We didn't have a line two, it just sounded good.

'Radio Boy! This show is what gets me through the week, but you gotta tell them who you are or you'll lose us all. I can't hear Elvis or the girl in the background – have they quit?'

Maybe I *had* lost sight of why I'd done this show in the first place. It certainly seemed like I'd lost the listeners.

'OK. Look, I . . .'

But whatever I was about to say was suddenly interrupted. The shed door shook violently.

Without any warning, it was then flung open with such force it was almost ripped off its hinges.

Right away Sherlock began barking at the crazed figure in the doorway. It was a masked madman yelling, 'GOTCHA! I KNOW WHO YOU ARE, RADIO BOY!'

CHAPTER 32

The UNMASKING

LIVE ON AIR, a madman had just burst in through the shed door and yelled, 'I KNOW WHO YOU ARE, RADIO BOY!'

A few things about this surprise development:

Round at Artie's house I'd seen some action movies (unapproved by Mum) where mid-fight-scene the hero pauses mid-punch and tells you what he's thinking. If I could have freeze-framed the scene before me as I sat there on my chair in the shed, here are a few things I would've noticed.

1. The madman was wearing a child's woollen ski mask stretched tightly over his massive face.
2. The person doing the yelling wasn't talking in a friendly 'Hey! Look who's here, it's Radio Boy, have some pizza,' kind of way. They seemed really, like, dangerously mad.
3. After the yelling, there was a familiar smell hanging like a stinky beef cloud in the shed.

But I didn't have long to process any of this.

1.7 seconds later, following the madman's sudden entrance, another hand was thrust in through the shed door. The hand then GRABBED the masked madman and YANKED him back out. The shed door slammed shut.

It was as if someone had just hit the rewind button.

I was aware I was still live on air, as well as

my life probably being under threat.

*'Er . . . I think I'm b-b-being attacked! Please
help me,'* was all I could stammer out.

I peered nervously through the dusty shed
window as the garden security lights came on,
illuminating two figures in my garden.

What happened next will be burned into my mind for eternity. And my life will forever be the better for it.

The owner of the yelling-madman-grabbing hand, the newest arrival to the scene, I could now see was most definitely Sensei Terry. Neighbourhood Watch vigilante, karate teacher and our trusty postman. A man of many hats.

His face tonight was not that of our friendly local postman, however, nor that of a protective Neighbourhood Watch member. It was a face I'd seen before in my own fateful karate lesson. This was Sensei Terry about to attack. He was defending me.

Finally, after twenty years of teaching karate to bored kids and overweight accountants, he was getting his chance to use his finely honed martial arts skills. This was the day he'd been training for, waiting for, praying for his entire life. This was going to be Sensei Terry's defining moment.

Sensei Terry's body was coiled like a cobra postman. The masked madman was about to meet the full force of the karate teacher's most feared move. The front kick.

In the one karate lesson I attended, this move proved too much for me and my sister's karate pants. But this was Sensei Terry. A master of this ancient art. His kick, after thousands of repetitions, was now like a finely oiled piston. The masked madman didn't stand a chance.

Piercing the night air was the war cry from Sensei Terry.

'MAE GERI!'

Even in battle, Sensei Terry was using the correct Japanese terminology. Maybe he was also summoning the spirit of ancient warriors who first used this fearsome move.

'MAE GERI!'

. . . and out it fired again.

His rear leg came up, powered by those hips

made so strong by years of carrying letters, parcels and my mum's seven-kilogram clothing catalogue. He flicked it out, and this time it rose high, not into the stomach of his opponent as I thought he intended, no: this time he'd set his kick on a different trajectory. Towards the face of the masked madman.

How can I best describe what happened next? If you've ever seen a watermelon explode, then that.

Sensei Terry's right foot met the masked madman's face and reorganised it. A front tooth came flying out and the man screamed in agony as he slumped to the ground. Perfect technique by Sensei Terry. I half expected him to bow.

Lots of things then happened at the same time.

The noise of Sensei Terry's blood-curdling 'MAE GERI!' war cry had obviously got some of my family's attention as they settled down to watch TV for the evening. As had the now-murmuring cries of the fallen, tooth-missing masked madman.

Dad came flying out into the garden.

Then my sister.

Then my mum.

I was still watching this box office movie from the shed window, for the moment not even remembering that my mic was live.

All anyone still listening to the *Secret Shed Show* would've heard was: '*Oh no. My mum! It's all over now.*'

Dad spoke first.

'Terry?' he said, peering into the floodlit garden that was now also an arena of Japanese combat.

'Yes, Mr and Mrs Hughes. Do not be alarmed, but I have just apprehended a masked intruder in your garden. You are in no danger from him now.' And to reinforce this point he gave a little nudge to the blood-masked, tooth-missing madman.

Sensei Terry continued his eyewitness report.

'. . . at approximately 5.57pm tonight I was making my usual rounds in my capacity as a member of our Neighbourhood Watch security team. I investigated a noise from your hedges, Mr Hughes. It was then I saw this person with binoculars, spying on your shed. Following this, I saw him try to get into it, whereupon I gave pursuit and pulled him out as he was yelling at someone inside.'

'Right . . .' said Dad, trying to put together the pieces of this bizarre jigsaw.

The blood-masked, tooth-missing madman began murmuring again and pointing towards the shed. Towards me.

'Oh, my poor boy, Spike! Is he still alive in there? Working on his mummy's birthday present, you BEAST!' Mum yelled at the blood-masked, tooth-missing madman.

Mum began to sprint towards me in the shed.

Oh no. Oh no, no, no, no.

'NO!' yelled Dad as Mum closed in on the shed and grasped the door handle.

Sensei Terry, meanwhile, was grappling to unmask the blood-masked, tooth-missing madman.

'Angel, are you OK in there?' cried my mum as yet again tonight the shed door was violently flung open.

'Um . . .'

'Spike? What's . . . all . . . this . . . equipment . . . What is all this stuff? Microphones . . . speakers . . .'

'Er . . .'

My mum processed everything in the shed and put it all together.

'It's a radio studio!!!!'

As if brought back to life by these words, the blood-masked, tooth-missing, mumbling madman suddenly found the bodily strength to peel off the overly tight ski mask. Despite being blood-splattered, missing a tooth and still looking demented, the madman was unmistakably visible for who he was.

It was Mr Harris, my headmaster. He had finally found Radio Boy.

Fish Face began shouting excitedly. Due to the state of his mouth and the fact that a tooth of his was somewhere in our rose bush, all that came out was *'nmph nadio toy . . . nadio toy'*.

Sensei Terry gave him another prod in the ribs to silence him.

Over Mum's shoulder I saw my dad's face: it was like he was watching a car crash about to happen. I also caught my sister's expression as she was trying to see beyond Mum and into the shed.

Mum spoke again.

'You're Radio Boy? You? My Spike?'

'Um. Yes.' I swallowed.

She narrowed her eyes. 'Who else knew?'

Dad braced himself for impact.

She looked over at him, and he looked down at his feet. She looked over at Mr Harris, back to me and then to the studio. She slammed the shed door closed in my face, as if to shut out the deception that was behind it. The force of it shook the entire shed, and our neighbourhood, possibly even registering 'small earthquake' on the Richter scale.

It all proved to be too much for the shed door, as it gave up and fell off into the garden. Leaving me in full view.

CHAPTER 33

The fallout

And then the police arrived.

They had kindly responded to several calls from my concerned listeners, but they were somewhat delayed as most of the callers could give my location only as 'a garden shed'. Luckily, one of them could, but strangely only gave his name as 'Elvis'.

The sight of them arresting Mr Harris and charging him with illegal trespassing was incredible, yet made perfect sense among the barely believable events of the weirdest day of my life.

As Fish Face was led away from my garden in handcuffs and put in the back of a police car, a familiar face appeared at the front door.

Derek Mountfield, there to get his big news scoop.

Mr Harris had sneakily telephoned Derek and told him to get to my house, because he was about to uncover the identity of Radio Boy. Mr Harris, unable to predict what would actually happen, had excitedly imagined that a juicy front cover was surely awaiting him in the local paper – perhaps a photo of him holding me up by the scruff of the neck. Like a hunter with his prize catch.

Derek Mountfield *did* get his second scoop of the day, but not the one Fish Face planned. Instead, it was a front-page snap of a local headmaster being handcuffed and put into the back of a police car yelling, 'HE'S THE CRIMINAL, NOT ME!'

Goodness knows how this will all be reported on Merit Radio, I thought.

I couldn't really enjoy that thought for too long as there was a gloomy silence now in my house after the drama of the last hour.

The atmosphere in the living room was, to say the least, 'strained'. How could it not be?

My mum had been lied to not only by her son, but her husband as well. She'd seen my headmaster break into our garden, be attacked by our postman and get arrested. And she'd discovered that her son had been broadcasting a secret show from the family shed. That her husband knew all about and had helped set it up. This was like one of those daytime TV shows my nan loves where angry-faced people with few or no teeth shout across a TV studio at each other, while a man in a suit sits on the studio floor, patronising them.

'Just go to your bedroom, son, I'll handle this,'

Dad said quietly. I'd never seen him so dejected.

'No, I think I need to do this, Dad.'

And I did. I felt really awful. Like the worst son in the world. I could be starring in my own episode of those daytime TV shows: *When Good Sons Go Bad.*

TV host in suit grinning into camera with perfect hair and super-white teeth.

'Coming up after the break, we meet this poor, hard-working mother of two who is a hospital ward manager.'

Cut to image of my mum smiling, maybe that holiday one of her in a sombrero despite the fact we weren't in Spain but camping.

'By day, caring for the sick; by night, BETRAYED BY HER SON with a secret radio show from their family shed.'

Cut to that school photo where I look like a crazed killer.

'Today: IS THIS THE WORST SON IN THE WORLD – EVER?'

As I went to find her, I thought about everything that had happened as a result of me going too far with the strike. Everything was my fault. I'd had it all, and now I'd ruined it all.

Great work, me!

As I got to Mum's bedroom, I could hear my sister in there already. No doubt sticking her unhelpful opinion in. Just *loving* her little brother being in DEEP, DEEP trouble. I was wrong though. As I hesitated outside the door, I heard Amber talking.

'You know what, Mum? I'm embarrassed sometimes that Spike's my brother.'

Oh, thanks for that, Amber.

But she carried on, and I stood there, stunned at what I heard.

'He acts so weird, but I had no idea that the

show everyone was talking about at school was being done by *my* little brother in *our* shed. I mean, him? I have to admit . . . I'm kinda proud. I'm pleased for him, Mum. He's still a freak, but saying that, how the hell did he even *do* it?'

I was amazed. Let's leave aside the fact she called me a 'freak' – this was still the kindest thing I'd ever heard my sister say, and for the first time that day I felt I had someone on my side.

Mum didn't say anything.

My sister opened the bedroom door. 'Good luck,' she offered as she gently patted me on the shoulder.

I smiled at her. 'Thanks.'

'Yeah, don't push it, weirdo,' she said, and walked away.

Here goes.

I knocked on the door and went in. My mum was sitting on her bed. Even just seeing her sitting down and not moving or holding court said how much this had knocked it out of her. For once, Carol Bond hadn't seen this one coming.

'I'm sorry, Mum,' I mumbled.

She looked up. Her big eyes were full of hurt. Not anger, like I expected, but hurt. That was even worse in a way.

'Why didn't you and your dad tell me?'

'Cos I thought you'd never let me do it.'

'Well. That makes me sad, Spike. That you think I'd not support your dreams.'

'You worry all the time though,' I said. 'What would people say? Could the equipment explode? Blowing my head clean off my shoulders into the neighbours' garden, leaving me with a fake head like some made-up patient you once treated on the ward.'

'I only want you and your sister to be safe! I do what I think is best for you,' she protested. 'If you'd seen the horrors I've seen, Spike, *you'd* be protective. Just yesterday a boy came in, had one of those hoverboards as a birthday present. It took him under a pig truck and now he has a tiny, tiny head and body after it was squished so badly. Poor kid will have to use Build-A-Bear outfits as clothing . . .'

'Mum . . .'

'OK, some of that I may have exaggerated.'

'I know, but . . . this *Secret Shed Show* was a risk, Mum. You'd have been worried about me getting into trouble.'

'Well, I would've been right to after what I've just seen. Mr Harris breaking into our garden! What have you done, Spike?'

I had nothing to say. It was my turn to look at my feet now.

'Sit down, Spike.' She patted the bed next to her. 'What upsets me the most, more than the lies that you and your dad told, and don't even get me started on your dad's part in all this . . . I'll deal with HIM LATER . . .'

Mum started to do that crazy-eyed, staring

thing she does, where her eyes bulge and she begins chewing her lip. She was back. Poor Dad. He'd be praying for a cell next to Fish Face after Mum was finished with him.

'No, what was I saying? Yes, what upsets me is why did you use the name *Radio Boy*? Why not be you?'

'Well, I guess because otherwise Mr Harris would've found out and stopped us.'

'But we wouldn't have let him. It's not illegal what you've been doing.'

Oh. I thought about that. She was right, I realised. Mr Harris couldn't *actually* stop us broadcasting. It was just an internet radio show.

'I didn't . . . think of it like that,' I said. 'I was just scared of him, I guess.'

'Is that really why you kept it secret?'

'Well . . .' I shrugged, awkwardly.

'Come on. What really stopped you, Spike? I'm curious.'

Mum put her arm round me. And it felt good. It had been an awful day. The first half amazing, second half the worst day of my life ever. The manhunt, losing Artie and Holly. Now the police were involved. There's something about a hug from your mum or dad when you really need it. I guess I wasn't really a superhero. Though I reckon even Batman would stop scowling for a bit if he had one of my mum's hugs.

'I thought . . .' I said, finally. 'That if I was just Spike Hughes no one would listen. Because I'm invisible at school, Mum. No one knows who I am. I'm not in the cool kids' gang, or *any* gang. So I kinda invented Radio Boy. Like a superhero. He was everything I'm not. Funny, brave, exciting.'

'You are all those things, Spike. You're the funniest person I know.'

'You always say that, but you're my mum, so you have to. It's like parent law. To all parents, their kids are great-looking and funny and clever.

No parent has ever gone, "Jeez, you're a bit of an ugly one, aren't you? And thick with it."'

Mum laughed at this. Maybe we would be all right.

'But I know it's true. And so do you now, if you think about it. Radio Boy is *you*, Spike. Everyone's been talking about how funny the show is, even the mums. He just woke something up that was always in there. He just helped you find that in you.'

'I dunno . . .'

'Look, I'm far from happy with what's gone on in the last few weeks, and I'm furious with your dad for allowing it to go this far and letting you get yourself in trouble with this strike, but—'

'Er, Mum, Dad didn't know anything about the strike.'

'He didn't?'

'No, that bit's all my fault. It was all my idea. Artie and Holly begged me not to do it.'

'Wow. Wow. I'm really surprised.'

'What do you mean?'

'Well, it was the wrong thing to do and we will have to think about what you need to do next, but it's also . . . pretty amazing.'

'Amazing? How?'

'That someone who thinks they're so rubbish managed to pull all this off and right under my nose. That's . . . seriously impressive. I can't even begin to imagine how you did it.'

'I had help.'

'I'm sure, but you made all this happen. Well, you surprised everyone, Spike Hughes.'

My heart swelled with joy and happiness.

'I guess you want me to stop doing the show now . . .' I said.

'Let's just wait for tonight to settle first. The police want us to go to the station first thing in the morning and we will have to speak to the school, and Artie's and Holly's parents.'

I got up, but as I was leaving her bedroom my mum had just one final thing to say.

'Have you been to the toilet today?'

CHAPTER 34

Too many apologies

Normally, weekends are pretty standard and boring for me. Might go round Artie's or Holly's to hang out, might do some homework. Walk Sherlock, throw some sticks for Sherlock, pick up Sherlock's poop. Avoid my sister and her pony, Mr Toffee, and do homework. Not this weekend though. This was no normal weekend. This was the morning after SHED ARMAGEDDON.

I was 'invited' by Dad to help him attach a

new shed door. I also saw that there was a newly installed camp bed in the shed where Dad was apparently now going to sleep for a few days, 'just until things settle down with your mum', he whispered, casually. As if this was a normal thing. It was obviously his punishment for his part in the crime of the century. Over the past few weeks, the shed had gone from being a place to dump the lawnmower to a radio studio, and now it was doubling up as a dad prison.

He'd probably quite enjoy it actually. I noticed he'd already tried to make it as cosy as possible. He had a few books in there with him, and some snacks Mum doesn't usually let him have – chocolate bars, cold pizza and beer. It looked like a friendly tramp had moved in.

All morning there were lots of 'chats' between Mum and Dad. When I say 'chats', I don't mean some calm and reasonable exchanges of opinions between two caring parents. I mean that special 'plane mode' arguing your mum and dad do when they think they can kid you they aren't actually having an argument by not raising their voices. It's whispered shouting. I could guess the main topic of the 'chats'.

Meanwhile, my phone was shaking every few minutes with texts. I'd never been so popular. They were asking if I was really Radio Boy. News spreads quickly, and news about the headmaster breaking into your garden, getting arrested and losing a tooth in the process spreads even quicker. Mum had told me not to speak to anyone until they (she) had worked out what was going to happen.

Then, when my sister came back from feeding money to her pony, she gave me news that broke my heart.

She came into my bedroom, reeking of hay and pony poop.

'I know who dobbed you in to Fish Face,' she said.

'WHO! Artie or Holly?' I guessed.

'No. You won't like this, but it was Katherine Hamilton, Spike.'

The room was spinning. I played back the memory of her calling the show.

'*You're the best.*'

Then I remembered Holly's words. 'She was using you . . . Like she does everyone.'

'I-I-I . . .' I stammered.

'I told you she was awful,' said Amber. 'She was down the stables, feeding her pony, Katherine Junior, and she saw me and walked right up and told me! She's evil, Spike. I know you have a crush on her, but you need to know the truth.'

I could hardly speak. 'Yes, yes, thanks,' I muttered. Spike or Radio Boy, I meant nothing to Katherine Hamilton. It was over.

After lunch, I was summoned by Dad to the dinner table, where a formal meeting was being held. Mum and Dad sat on one side of the table, me on the other. Like some special trial or hearing was about to take place. Mum had thoughtfully placed a bowl in the middle of the table with some fruit in, which she offered me. '*Good for your digestion.*'

Mum started the proceedings. This was scarier than the interrogation from Mr Harris. You never knew what my mum would come out with from moment to moment, and recent events would have sent her into overdrive.

'OK, the last twenty-four hours have been very hard on me, Spike. What you did, and your dad let you do . . .'

MUM SHOT DAD SOME SERIOUS SIDEWAYS STINK EYE AT THIS POINT. The power of the stink eye was ten times that of a laser beam; it froze Dad on the spot.

'While it was also very impressive, what you did with your show has caused some very serious problems that your dad and I have to deal with. That *you* will also have to deal with.'

If Mum's face was an emoji, it would look like this:

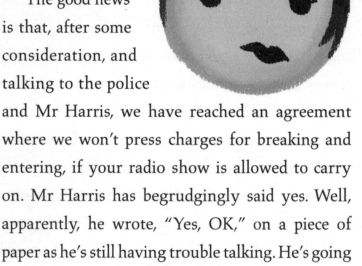

'The good news is that, after some consideration, and talking to the police and Mr Harris, we have reached an agreement where we won't press charges for breaking and entering, if your radio show is allowed to carry on. Mr Harris has begrudgingly said yes. Well, apparently, he wrote, "Yes, OK," on a piece of paper as he's still having trouble talking. He's going to be on a soup-only diet for the next few weeks. It seems he almost cried when he was told this, as it means no jumbo sausage rolls for a while.'

I started to smile, then immediately stopped when I saw Mum's face.

Next, it was Dad's turn to speak at the hearing.

'We have a few conditions, Spike. One . . .'

ONE? Gulp. How many would there be? Did I need a pen and paper to make notes?

'You will return the turntable you "borrowed" to the hospital radio station. Yes, we know all about that little heist, thank you, Spike. That's who tipped off Mr Harris, by the way, your old colleague Graham the—'

'Him as well?'

I could just imagine the gnome getting off the phone to Mr Harris, knowing full well that he had just given a bloodthirsty hound my scent. His round gnome belly shaking with sickening laughter as his head wobbled, maybe dislodging a small nesting rodent from his overgrown beard.

'You will apologise to Graham—'

'WHAT!' I yelled, spitting the words out.

'You will,' said Mum, calmly. Then she dropped the big one.

'And you will go and apologise to Mr Harris.'

'NO! PLEASE, COME ON!'

'You will or no more radio show. Are we clear?'

'OK, right.' Just the very thought of it made me shudder and want to throw up.

'One last point, and it's the most important of the lot,' Mum added. 'This is all about doing the right thing. In life, we sometimes have to take responsibility for our actions, and that's a lesson you are learning this weekend. Your two best friends tried to stop you going ahead with the strike idea, and you should've listened. You need to make it up with them. Good friends are hard to come by.'

'Yeah,' was all I could offer.

'I don't know anything about how radio works, but these . . . customers who listen—'

'Listeners, Mum, they're called listeners,' I interrupted firmly (but very, very gently, given my weak position).

'Yes, that's what I meant. Well, just like Artie and Holly, you have to do right by those listeners too. They are your friends, in a way, and when you asked them to take a stand and strike, they did. You need to make your own stand now.'

'What do you mean?'

'I think you know.'

And I did.

CHAPTER 35

Do the right thing

I texted Artie and Holly.

> TUNE IN TONIGHT AT 6.
> SPECIAL SHOW. PLEASE LISTEN.

I posted the same message on the *Secret Shed Show* website and Facebook. That night, as I headed down to the shed, past the battlefield where Mr Harris and Sensei Terry had fought, I looked back, and I saw Mum and Dad watching me from separate windows. Mum nodded and Dad gave his trademark thumbs-up. I looked towards my sister's window. Nothing. Then I saw the pony-themed curtains peel back, and her face appeared. She smiled at me. Slightly. It was the best I could hope for from her.

I did all my usual pre-show checks. The voice disguiser on, records cued and ready, mics checked, then as the studio clock struck six I opened the mic and spoke.

'Hi, this is Radio Boy here on the *Secret Shed Show*. So, where do I begin? Well, first by doing this . . .'

I leant over and turned *off* the voice disguiser.

'When I started this show, I felt something I'd never felt before in my life. That I was good at something. I'd finally found what I was good at. What I was meant to do. Felt a part of my own gang. Then I got carried away with my new powers. Sorry about that. I hope one day we can have a laugh about it. I thought I could only do this by hiding who I really was, that I was boring and Radio Boy wasn't. He was a superhero. But I've learned something. We all have a superpower in us. You don't need a cape, just courage. The courage to take a risk, to follow your dream.

'So . . .

'What I want to say is . . .

'My name is Spike Hughes, and I'm Radio Boy.'

CHAPTER 36

The dream team rides again

I played a song. Then another. I was too busy reading messages from listeners that were pouring in. Supporting me for owning up. Tears were flooding my eyes. Happy tears.

Then the shed door opened.

'You still need a producer?' asked Holly.

'You *definitely* need a head of music,' said Artie. 'That last song stank so badly you might want to open a window in here.'

I laughed.

The adventure could carry on.

To be continued . . .

Note from me, the writer of this, Spike Hughes

Thanks for buying my book.* You should know that if I do, like, make any cash from this I'm going to spend it on:

- A new microphone.
- Better soundproofing for the shed studio, an upgrade of the egg-box cartons.
- A new dog bed for Sherlock.

So thanks. I'll be honest: writing this book was a massive pain in the backside. It was another one of Mum and Dad's 'conditions' when they said I could carry on with the show.

'You should write it all down, son, the whole

* If you stole this book then I'm telling Sensei Terry on you.

story. One day you'll forget how it all started,' said Dad.

If there are any spelling mistakes in this then remember I'M A KID. You see many successful books written by kids? Exactly.

Radio is my thing. Not this. You don't get to have two superpowers.

If you've managed to make it to the end of this book, then I hope that, before you throw it in the bin, you think about what your superpower is. Big, small, weird, odd: doesn't matter. Fear and doubt kill dreams; don't let them kill yours. Even if you make a giant fool of yourself like I did, then at least you'll have a great story to tell people.

Email me if you want at radioboy@ radioboy.co.uk.

I gotta go – I have a radio show to get ready for.

Radio Boy
AKA
Spike Hughes

Acknowledgements

To my wife Sarah. My biggest fan and my biggest critic. For telling me to try harder and for having better ideas than mine.

My daughters Ruby and Lois. The mini-editors of this book. Who would hand me back chapters with notes on them like, *'I DON'T THINK THIS IS VERY FUNNY,'* and, *'GIVE UP.'* In all seriousness, you two laughing will always be the greatest sound in the world. Thanks for all your help. – *Dad*

Rob Biddulph for his amazing illustrations.

Nick Lake. My grown-up Editor. Who said, *'I just have a few notes'* and sent me a document eleven pages long. Your support and faith from day one helped make this book whatever it is. So if it's funny, that's your help, if it tanks, you're fired. Take your notes with you.

My Harper Heroes: Ann-Janine Murtagh,

Kate Clarke, Elorine Grant, Jane Tait, Jo Hardacre, Tanya Brennand-Roper and everyone in the Sales and Marketing teams who has worked so hard to bring *Radio Boy* to the world.

Melanie and Dylan at Troika. For telling me there might be something in that idea you've been boring us with for a few years.

Mr Taggart. Mr Taggart was an actual teacher of mine. He sat me down one day after school and told me to go and do something 'making people laugh'. This was a big deal for a school loser like me. He set a lightbulb off in me that I will always be thankful for. I never got the chance to say thank you because he passed away. Putting him in this book is a small way of me doing that.